Books by Pat Posner
in the Linford Romance Library:

PRESCRIPTION FOR HAPPINESS
SUNLIGHT ON SHADOWS
TANGLED WEB
ROMANCE IN THE AIR
A SONG ON THE JUKEBOX

A SURPRISE ENGAGEMENT

Flora can't understand how she let her best friend, Val, persuade her to pretend to be engaged to Val's brother, Bryce Torman, heir to the Torman estate. It's only supposed to convince their Uncle Hector that Bryce is serious about someone other than the singing star, Jilly Joy, he's recently been spotted with. To make matters worse, Flora and Bryce have got on like chalk and cheese since childhood — and yet Flora finds herself enjoying his 'fake' kisses rather more than she ought to . . .

PAT POSNER

A
SURPRISE
ENGAGEMENT

Complete and Unabridged

LINFORD
Leicester

First published in Great Britain in 2017

First Linford Edition
published 2018

C46378409A

A catalogue record for this book is available
from the British Library.

ISBN 978–1–4448–3582–3

Published by
F. A. Thorpe (Publishing)
Anstey, Leicestershire

Set by Words & Graphics Ltd.
Anstey, Leicestershire
Printed and bound in Great Britain by
T. J. International Ltd., Padstow, Cornwall

This book is printed on acid-free paper

1

'You can't be serious, Val. Waking me on a Sunday morning and asking me to . . .'

Flora stumbled out of bed and, half-wondering whether she was dreaming, followed her friend, who was walking purposefully into the living room. Rubbing sleep-laden eyes, she made her way over to the large window. 'I thought All Fools' Day was April the First, not December the First,' she muttered as she stretched her arms up to pull back the heavy gold curtains, expecting to see the marvellous view across to the local cricket ground her top-floor flat afforded.

She gasped at what met her eyes and pivoted around to face her friend. 'Good grief, it's even earlier than I thought. It's still dark out there. What time is it? Shift yourself, Val; I can't see the clock.'

'Not much point in looking at it when you never have it set to the right time,' said Val. 'It's just coming up to seven o'clock,' she added, glancing at her watch.

Flora shook her head. 'Only something desperate could get you out of bed so early on a Sunday and make you drive over here. So it isn't some kind of joke. You *are* serious.'

'Of course I'm serious. Flora, you've got to do it. You see . . . ' Val jumped as the telephone shrilled. 'That'll be Uncle Hector. I knew he'd phone to ask you if it's true. Tell him it is. Please, Flora. And don't let him know I'm here — I'll explain everything afterwards, I promise.'

Much against her better judgement, but unable to ignore the deeply worried look on her best friend's face, Flora sighed. 'All right. But it had better be good,' she warned, eyeing Val as she swept past her to get to the phone, which was situated in the hall. 'And I think it might help if you get some coffee going. Something tells me I'm going to need a few cups.'

A few minutes later, after replacing the telephone receiver back on its rest, Flora acknowledged ruefully to herself that it would take more than a few cups of coffee to make any sense of what she'd just admitted to.

'Well?' demanded Val, hovering in the kitchen doorway. 'Did Uncle Hector believe you?'

'*Gullible* and *dim* aren't words I'd normally use to describe your uncle Hector,' Flora replied dryly, 'but surprisingly, I think he did.'

'That's all right then.' Val's breath hissed out in a sigh of what Flora guessed was sheer relief.

'No, Val, it isn't all right at all.' Flora ran her fingers through her hair, still tousled from sleeping, and glared at her friend. 'I've just let your uncle think that your brother and I are secretly engaged. How the heck he could believe that when Bryce and I fight like cat and dog whenever we meet . . . And Bryce?

3

Where is he? Does he know about this . . . this . . . ?' Flora broke off to groan as the full enormity of the situation hit her. Hard. 'What on earth have I done, and why have I done it? You'd better start explaining, Val.'

'Go back into the living room and read this.' Val pulled a newspaper from the pocket of the duffel coat she was still wearing and thrust it towards Flora. 'I'll pour the coffee and bring it through.'

The newspaper — one of the less salubrious — had been folded to reveal the 'Sunday Snippet' column. Staring down at a picture of Bryce, Flora walked slowly into the living room.

The photographer had captured his very essence, she noted. Dynamic, and so attractive and appealing. Not that Bryce appealed to *her* in the slightest. Her increased heart rate was down to being woken so rudely by Val and allowing herself, whilst still half-asleep, to get dragged into this crazy ploy.

No, these days Bryce's rather obvious

attractions — long, lean body honed to physical perfection, thick black hair, dark eyes, that lazy half-smile, the hard angle of his beautifully sculpted jaw — didn't set her heart racing at all. Not so the woman in the picture, though. She was staring up at Bryce with a sickeningly adoring look.

'Oh well, there's no accounting for taste,' murmured Flora as she sat down to read the so-called snippet. 'Is Bryce Torman about to become Mr Jilly Joy number three?' shrieked the caption. *Can't see her in wellies wandering around the farming estates in the middle of winter,* Flora thought acidly, before reading on: 'Scotland's number-one singing star, Jilly Joy, recently divorced from husband number two, was spotted dancing the night away with Bryce Torman (33), the probable heir to his uncle's dynasty. Hector Torman is one of the country's wealthiest land-owners. Coincidentally, Jilly Joy will soon be appearing in a musical show close to Bryce's home in the county of Derby-shire. When asked about her relationship with Bryce Torman, Jilly replied joyfully: 'We're close friends.'

'See? Now do you understand, Flora?' demanded Val, pushing a cup of coffee into her friend's hand.

'Less than ever.'

'Oh, come on, Flora. Think. You know what Uncle Hector can be like. He's scarcely likely to approve of Bryce getting mixed up with someone like Jilly Joy.'

'But Bryce is *always* getting mixed up with someone in the limelight. And always getting his name in the gossip columns.'

'Exactly.' Val nodded her head emphatically. 'And last time it happened, Uncle Hector gave Bryce one last chance. Said if he didn't turn over a new leaf and stop foisting unwelcome publicity on the family, he'd disinherit him and make our cousin Rupert his heir.'

'In that case, Bryce should be more careful about being seen dancing the night away with someone whose very lifestyle gives the gossip columnists something to gossip about.' Flora drained her coffee cup, banged it down on a nearby table, and leapt to her feet. 'Just tell me, Val, how did my name get into all this?'

'Well, Bryce's playboy reputation is grossly exaggerated. He can't go anywhere, or do anything, without somebody — '

'Get to the point,' Flora bit out, waving the newspaper in front of Val's face. 'I presume your uncle read this snippet and was unable to vent his rage on Bryce because Bryce is somewhere with his 'close friend', so you were the recipient — '

'He phoned me at quarter to six. You know Uncle Hector always gets up early, though it beats me how he manages to get his newspapers delivered at that — '

'Va-a-l.'

'All right, all right, I'm trying to get to the point. Just stop glowering at me, Flora. When you do that, I can't think straight.'

'You can say that again. You weren't thinking straight when you told your uncle that Bryce and I are secretly engaged.' Flora waved the newspaper again. 'Can't you see if that were true, it would make this even worse?'

'No. That's the whole point. Because you're secretly engaged, it proves the article is just vicious gossip. Whatever his faults, Bryce isn't dishonourable.'

'Hmm. Maybe not,' Flora said.

'Definitely not. Even Uncle Hector is willing to admit that. Look, Bryce was only clubbing with Jilly Joy last weekend because he was staying at her parents' farm in Scotland. He wants to buy some of their Highland cattle. He left Scotland on Monday morning and flew out to the States to do a series of lectures on organic farming. But he's due back this morning. In . . . ' She glanced at the time. ' . . . an hour and a half.'

Ignoring the parts she thought irrelevant, Flora snapped, 'Apart from the mere detail that it would be unlikely for Bryce to see Highland cattle in a night club, why didn't you point out the salient facts to your uncle? After all, he must have known why Bryce was in Scotland, must have known where Bryce was staying.'

'I tried all that. Uncle Hector wouldn't listen. Said there was no smoke without fire, and Bryce had just used his last match, and this time he darned well would disinherit him. That's when my brilliant idea hit me.'

'But why did you have to cast me as Bryce's secret fiancée?'

Val sighed. 'Because you're my best friend?'

Flora snorted. 'If that's supposed to be friendship, I'd hate to be your enemy.'

'Okay, I couldn't think of anyone else suitable enough,' admitted Val.

'You're seeing the world through rose-coloured glasses, Val. There's no way Bryce would consider me suitable, not even for a fake engagement.'

'Well, I know you always manage to start an argument with him, but that doesn't make you unsuitable.'

'I don't mean because we argue, but . . . but because we come from different backgrounds.'

'Flora, that's tosh. Bryce doesn't care a fig about that sort of thing.'

Yup, rose-coloured glasses, thought Flora. True, it didn't seem to matter to Bryce when it came to him having one of his infamous flings. But anything else . . .

'It wouldn't be fair if Bryce lost his inheritance,' Val continued. 'Oh, I know he enjoys social life but he also works hard. He gives his all to the Torman Estate; he always has. You were part of our childhood, you saw how hard Bryce worked even then.'

Flora had to admit that was true. She'd been six when her recently widowed mother was offered the position of personal assistant to Hector Torman. A cottage on the estate went with the job, but working hours were spent in Torman Hall itself, so it soon became Flora's home after school and during the school holidays.

She had quickly become best friends with Val, Hector Torman's niece, who lived at the Hall while her parents were abroad. Friends with Val and enemies with Val's brother, Bryce. But even then at fifteen, when not tormenting the two younger girls, Bryce had worked hard, going out in all weathers with his uncle to check stock and visit the various far-spread farms on the estate and getting up early to do farm work before going to school.

Later, he'd gone to agricultural college. Then, after a couple of months at home, he had spent a year in Australia. When he'd finally come back to take up permanent residence in his own self-contained wing of the Hall, Flora began to see him through different eyes. He'd become her fantasy, her idol, her knight on a white charger. But that fantasy hadn't lasted for long, and she didn't want to remember that period of her life anyway.

Now, another eight years on, and more deliciously attractive than ever, he had women falling over themselves for his attention. But not her. The only thing Bryce aroused in her was . . . was . . .Well, she couldn't think of a word to describe it, but it certainly wasn't a yearning for his company. Everyone at Torman Hall knew the two of them couldn't spend five minutes together without disagreeing about something or other. But in spite of that, Hector Torman somehow, some way, actually believed she and his nephew were secretly engaged.

And Bryce, knowing nothing of this, would soon be home.

'You do realise, Val, that when Bryce arrives, your uncle is going to congratulate him on his engagement? But it's so secret even Bryce himself doesn't know about it. That's really brilliant. Can't you imagine your brother's reaction when he hears he's supposed to be engaged to *me*? It doesn't bear thinking about. And why are we supposed to have kept it secret anyway?'

The telephone shrilling out halted

Flora's tirade for a moment, but didn't calm her down. Flouncing towards the living room door, she warned over her shoulder, 'If that's your uncle Hector again, I'm going to tell him it was all a ridiculous joke, a trick, a lie, a . . .'

After a while, Flora exploded back into the room. 'That was my mother. Your uncle phoned her and she's over the moon at the fantastic news. She said she wasn't surprised because she's always known Bryce and I were meant for each other, and she knew it was only a matter of time before we realised it ourselves.'

'Oh,' said Val.

' 'Oh,'' mimicked Flora. 'Is that all you can say? And I suppose I'll have your mother on the phone any minute as well.'

'You won't. I told Uncle Hector not to tell her. Er . . . you didn't tell your mum it isn't true, did you?'

'I didn't get the chance. It's pointless trying to get a word in when Mum's excited. After talking wedding dress and

13

bridesmaids, and bemoaning the fact that there won't be time for us to arrange a double wedding with you and Quentin, she said she'd start making lists and bring them with her to your party tonight.'

'Your mum and her lists,' murmured Val.

Flora waggled a finger under her friend's nose. 'Perhaps you should start a list. A list of possible answers as to why Bryce and I have kept our engagement a secret. Because Mum said she couldn't understand why we'd done that. Still at least, before she hung up, she promised she wouldn't tell anyone.'

'Wedding,' Val said. 'My wedding is so close. That's why . . . Yes, that's why you and Bryce wanted to keep your engagement secret. You didn't want to steal any of my limelight. You thought it wouldn't be fair if you announced it with Quentin and me getting married in — '

'Now, listen, Val, and listen good.

14

Even if Bryce already knew about this . . . this ridiculous idea of yours, there's no way we can carry it off. Nobody is going to believe it.'

'My uncle and your mother already do,' Val pointed out. 'And my mother will be only too glad to believe it. She adores you, you know she does.'

'Well, it's all immaterial anyway.' Flora's temper fizzled out and she threw herself on to the sofa and laughed. 'Bryce will give it away the very second your uncle mentions it, and then the two of you will have a lot of explaining to do. You know what? I can almost feel sorry for Bryce. He certainly won't have been expecting a surprise engagement as a welcome-home.'

'You won't need to feel sorry for him,' said Val. 'My idea might have hit me like a bolt from the blue, but it is workable.' And, with frequent glances at the time, she went on to explain how they could make it work.

2

Flora lay back in the air bath — a luxury she'd been unable to resist having installed when she'd bought the flat three years ago with some of the money that had been placed in trust for her until she was twenty-one. Strangely, although he'd been unable to resist a couple of his awful puns, it had been Bryce who'd supported her when her mother had queried the wisdom of spending so much on a fancy bath. Because, after buying her flat, there'd been enough of the trust money left for Flora to set up her first Flower Boutique, Daisy Chain.

And, as Bryce had pointed out — after commenting she ought to call her boutique Flora's *Floral* Boutique — she'd be making a round trip of over fifty miles two or three times a week to collect fresh flowers from the market. She'd be getting up at the crack of dawn, going out in all weathers, then coming back to stand in a cold outhouse at the back of her shop to sort the flowers and make up bouquets. If Flora wanted to splash out on an air bath to relax in after work, it seemed a sensible precaution against aching joints and muscles, Bryce had concluded with a charming smile for Mrs Grant.

Flora was far from feeling relaxed at the moment. In fact, she knew she was deliberately letting her mind wander in order to keep it off the forthcoming confrontation. How had she allowed Val to talk her into the absurd pretence of being engaged to Bryce?

No matter what Val had said before dashing off to pick him up from the airport, he'd never agree to this crazy scheme. But off her friend had gone, saying that instead of driving Bryce to Torman Hall, as he'd be expecting her to, she'd be bringing him here. Flora wriggled fretfully. Even if he did agree to the subterfuge, they'd never be able

17

to carry it off, never be able to act the part of a couple in love.

Love! Flora thought derisively. *I thought Harvey and I were in love, and look what happened there.* Okay, she was willing to accept love existed for some people — given she was a florist, it was lucky for her it did. At least it helped her make a good living. As for love in her personal life . . . Well, the only thing Cupid seemed to send her was a poisoned arrow. She'd scrubbed the L-word from her agenda.

How on earth would she be able to play the part of being happily engaged, especially to someone like Bryce? All she felt for him was . . . was . . . Finding herself still at a loss for a suitable word, she sighed as once again she heard the insistent shrilling of the telephone. She'd forgotten to switch it over to answerphone.

Well, she'd just ignore it. It would soon stop. But it didn't. Guessing it was probably her mother, who refused to call anyone on their mobile phone number unless it was an emergency, and also refused to send text messages — and knowing her mother wouldn't hang up until the phone cut itself off, Flora jumped out of the bath, snatched up a towel and, wrapping it round herself, hurried into the hall.

Her guess had been right. And Flora emphasised the fact that she'd got out of the bath to answer the phone, and was dripping all over the hall carpet. But her mother, after reminding Flora to use the special shampoo she'd bought her for honey-blonde hair — 'It will bring out your golden highlights' — went on to talk about her plans for an engagement party. 'When the need for secrecy is over, of course.' Other than putting the receiver down — and Flora couldn't quite bring herself to do that — there was nothing she could do except stand there and listen whilst regretting that she'd never got round to changing over to cordless phones in the flat.

When she heard the sound of a key

turning in the front door lock, Flora realised just how long her mother had been burbling away to her. For the second time that morning, she cursed the fact that Val always kept a key to the flat.

It was hard to stay calm and to find a way of stemming her mother's flow when Bryce's broad shoulders and towering body seemed to fill the hall; when she was sure she could feel his amused gaze on the bath towel. She gestured wildly towards the living room, wondering why he always appeared taller than the six foot one she knew he was, and tried not to react when his fingers reached out and squeezed her wet hair, causing uncomfortable drips to trickle down her back. But his whispered 'You look good enough to spread on bread' annoyed her far more than his action had done.

Somehow she managed to tell her mother she couldn't talk any longer. That was a laugh, seeing as her mother had been doing all the talking. And somehow she managed not to bang the receiver back onto its rest. But even the fact that she was wearing only a towel didn't prevent her from tearing into the living room and rounding furiously on Bryce. 'It's bad enough you being here without you making fun of my name.'

'Ah, yes, I remember.' Bryce grinned. Then he mimicked a Flora from their younger days. ''My *proper* name is Fleur.' That's what you used to say when I called you Flora vegetable spread. After that you usually told me to get lost.'

'You getting lost sounds good to me,' Flora told him. 'If you honestly think I'll go along with Val's totally crazy plan — '

'I've already told my dear sister that she can forget the whole idea,' Bryce snapped.

'That's the most sensible thing you've said in your entire life. Now I suggest you get out of my flat and go and face the music.'

'On balance, I'd rather face a five-foot pack of vegetable spread wrapped in a towel than — '

'Oh, for heaven's sake.' At last Val came to life, springing away from the window ledge against which she'd been leaning as an interested spectator. 'Won't you two ever grow up? Don't you realise how serious this whole thing is?'

At the sound of his sister's voice, Bryce turned to look at her. Flora took the opportunity to dash out of the room, calling loudly, 'And I'll have you know, Bryce Torman, I'm five foot *two*.'

★ ★ ★

Twenty minutes later, there came a tentative knock on Flora's bedroom door, followed by Val's subdued voice saying she'd made some more coffee.

Feeling calmer now, dressed in her favourite close-fitting jeans — because she liked them and not because they made her look taller — and a soft woollen jumper, her hair dried, therapeutically brushed and flowing over her shoulders in controlled waves, Flora opened the door and walked out. 'Living room or kitchen?' she asked coolly.

'Living room. Bryce lit the fire while I made the coffee. I'll just fetch the tray. You go on in.'

'Whose flat is this?' Flora muttered. But as she obeyed her friend's instruction, she felt her lips twitch in unwilling amusement.

Bryce had his back to her. He was standing by the window, presumably admiring the view, thought Flora. He turned as she walked across to the fire, and to her surprise he looked worried, the thick dark brows that bridged his midnight-blue eyes drawn together, his forehead wrinkled.

'What's wrong with Val?' he asked abruptly. 'It's something more than that stupid tittle-tattle in the paper.'

'Because of that tittle-tattle, your uncle was . . . is going to disinherit you.' Flora spoke patiently, as if to a child. 'Val didn't think you deserved that. She came up with what she thought was a good idea to protect you.'

Flora reached for the fire tongs, then crouched down to rearrange some pieces of coal. 'Now that we've refused to go along with that idea, she'll be angsting about having to tell your uncle and my mother that she invented the whole thing. Luckily, she asked Hector not to tell *your* mother.'

'So I believe,' he said tightly.

'Well, that'll be one less explanation for her.' Flora glanced over her shoulder at Bryce and added, 'If you both leave as soon as you've had a cup of coffee and go and explain things to your uncle, he'll have a few hours to simmer down before tonight's party.'

'There's something else, I know there is.' Bryce ran his fingers through his thick hair and sighed. 'If only I wasn't so tired, I'd be able to think better.'

About to come up with a sarcastic comment as to why he felt so tired, Flora opened her mouth, then bit firmly on her lower lip when she saw genuine concern in Bryce's eyes. 'Do you think your uncle will really carry out his threat this time?' she asked after a short silence.

'Disinherit me?' Bryce shrugged. 'Depends whether he believes I was only with Jilly because her parents asked me to escort her. Trouble is, I've promised to keep an eye on her while she's down here for the show. However, at the moment I'm more bothered about — ' He broke off as his sister came in and strode over to relieve her of the tray she was carrying. Flora shifted some magazines from the coffee table before going to sit in her favourite armchair.

'I made some toast as well.' Val sat down opposite Flora. 'I don't know about you two, but I'm starving.' Val's brightness sounded false and Flora wondered if Bryce was right. Maybe there was something else.

'I'm sure your uncle will understand when you explain things to him, Val.'

Flora studied her friend's face and didn't like what she saw. 'I'll explain to my mother, so don't worry about that,' she added.

A spurt of hysterical laughter burst from Val's mouth before she croaked, 'This might sound selfish, but at the moment I'm more worried about telling everyone that my wedding is off than explaining why I lied about you two being engaged.'

Flora stiffened, her hand arrested mid-air over the plate of toast Bryce was holding towards her. 'What are you talking about, Val? I don't believe this. You'd have told me earlier if something was wrong between you and Quentin.'

'I'm telling you now. There won't be a wedding. Quentin and I will not be getting married in twenty-seven days.' A tear trickling down Val's face added credence to her statement.

'Something doesn't add up here,' said Flora, looking at Bryce.

He nodded in agreement; then they turned their gaze to Val when she made a small mewling sound, both moving over to her chair as she buried her face in her hands.

'Since when has your wedding been off?' Bryce hunkered down in front of his sister and pulled her hands down.

Val's voice wobbled as she replied, 'I suppose since you saw fit to ignore Uncle Hector's warning and get your photo taken with a twice divorced woman said to be on the lookout for husband number three.'

'Val, you're overreacting.' Flora crouched down next to Bryce. 'You don't honestly think someone as nice, as honest, as true as your Quentin would abandon you because there's a possibility Bryce won't be inheriting the Torman Estate.'

'No, of course he wouldn't. But I can't let him go ahead with marrying me, not if it means . . . Oh, you don't understand.'

'I think I'm beginning to.' Bryce sounded grim. 'Just who is the very important business colleague Quentin is bringing to the party tonight?'

27

'Bryce. Don't worry her with silly questions like that,' Flora said. 'What does it matter who he's bringing?'

'Answer me, Val.' Bryce completely ignored Flora's words and looked hard at his sister.

'Someone from the Middle East or somewhere like that. Quentin is negotiating a very important deal with him. Contracts are due to be signed just before the wedding.'

'Now I see.' Bryce rose to his feet. 'Any unsavoury scandal, whether true or false, could affect the deal.'

'That's crazy.' Flora reached up and shook Val's shoulders. 'Quentin is marrying you, not your brother.'

'Unfortunately,' said Bryce, 'where Quentin's colleague comes from, they don't quite see things the same way as we do. In their eyes Quentin will be marrying the whole family. They wouldn't want to do business with someone who's related to a man who's thought to be involved with a woman who collects and discards husbands.'

'You mean because you and Jilly Joy have been seen together, because your name's linked with hers . . . ' Flora shook her head. 'You can't be serious, Bryce.'

'They could quite easily call the whole deal off on moral grounds,' he replied tersely.

'It's the biggest deal Quentin's ever handled,' Val said. 'Okay, I know he wouldn't give me up just to ensure it went through, so I'll have to be the one to cancel the wedding.'

'Val, listen — ' began Flora.

Bryce roughly pushed Flora aside and glared down at Val. 'So, little sister, the reason you thought up your plan wasn't a totally unselfish one? Only we weren't supposed to know that.'

'I — ' began Val.

Bryce's glare quietened her. 'Everything would have been fine if Flora and I had allowed you to pull the strings,' he continued. 'Quentin could have told his colleague Flora and I were engaged, the tit-bit in the paper would have been put down to vicious gossip, the deal would have gone ahead, and all would have been rosy in your garden — leaving Flora and me to get 'un-engaged' at some convenient time in the future.'

'It made sense,' Val said. 'And it would have been to your benefit too, Bryce. Uncle Hector was livid when he phoned me. He really meant it about disinheriting you. And I did stress the point that it was a secret engagement. You could have broken it off when the Jilly Joy thing died down without either you or Flora losing face, because nobody outside the family would have known about it.'

'Except Quentin's colleague. The real reason behind your plan,' Bryce reminded her harshly.

'Stop bullying her, Bryce.' Flora flew to her friend's defence. 'She's not asking that much of us, for heaven's sake. We'll be in each other's company all over Christmas anyway, what with the usual party for the estate workers and then the wedding a few days after that.'

'Let me get this straight, Flora.' Bryce swung towards her and gripped her shoulders, staring down into her face. 'Are you actually suggesting that we go along with this idea and pretend we're engaged?'

Flora slapped his hands away. 'I dislike the idea as much as you do,' she assured him. 'But yes, I'm suggesting we pretend to be engaged. Secretly engaged. We won't tell anyone outside the family except this contact of Quentin's we're meeting tonight. I don't care if your uncle disinherits you, but I do care about Val marrying the man she loves. And if you've got an ounce of brotherly feeling in you, you should care about that, too.'

Flora conveniently forgot that she'd told herself earlier that there was no way she could act the part of being happily engaged to Bryce. Val was her best friend; they were closer than sisters. The fact Val hadn't confided in her — hadn't even hinted Quentin's business deal could be in jeopardy if

Bryce was thought to be involved with a woman with a bad reputation — hurt.

But now she came to think of it, when Val had been talking about her wedding, it had sounded as if she was going to say something and then decided against it. Knowing Val, she'd probably been desperately trying to avoid what she would see as using their close bonds as emotional blackmail.

True, Val had played on their friendship when persuading her to pretend she and Bryce were engaged, Flora acknowledged. But none of that mattered now. If pretending to be engaged to Bryce meant Val could go ahead and marry Quentin, well, that was all that mattered.

'I won't plead with you, Bryce,' she told him. 'But surely you can see it would be a way of saving Val from heartache.'

'All right, we'll do it.' Bryce's words seemed to send electrical currents all round the room. 'After all, it won't be the first time you've pretended there's something between us, will it?'

3

Trust Bryce to remind me how pathetic I was at fifteen, thought Flora. She knew she was blushing with embarrassment, but stayed still and silent, determined not to react to his words.

'Okay,' said Bryce, apparently recognising the stubborn set to her mouth. 'Let's not dredge up the past. We should be thinking of the present and the future. Shall we seal our bargain with a kiss, Flora?'

Flora stepped back so quickly she almost fell over the coffee table.

'Was it such a terrible idea?' asked Bryce.

'Our bargain doesn't give you the right to torment me, Bryce.'

Val giggled. 'You used to call him Bryce *Torment* when we were little, remember?'

'I remember,' Flora replied quietly.

The trouble was, the threatened kiss had resurrected too much of the past. She could bury unwanted memories inside herself when Bryce was just a distant figure, but for the next few weeks he'd be far from that . . . Heavens, it didn't bear thinking about.

'I mean it, Bryce. We won't be able to pull this off if you torment me like you used to.'

'You did a fair amount of it yourself, Flora.' Bryce's voice was husky, and Flora had the feeling that he too was having trouble shutting out one particular memory. 'But, okay,' he added. 'For the sake of our engagement — ' He made inverted comma signs with his fingers. ' — we'll agree on no winding each other up.'

'You know what?' Val jumped up and stood facing Flora. 'It's a shame, really, that it's got to be a secret engagement. After what he said about you, what a poke in the eye it would be for Harvey Illingworth if he heard about it.'

'I think Bryce would probably agree

with Harvey. Just because I've got three flower boutiques and half-own a floral designing business in London, it doesn't make me — ' Flora broke off as she felt the bitter taste of bile rise at the back of her throat. 'Anyway,' she managed to add in a tone that showed she meant it, 'if you mention Harvey again in any context whatsoever, Val, I'll call this whole thing off.'

★ ★ ★

Seeing the look of hurt on Flora's face, and hearing it in her voice, made Bryce want to put his arms around her and hold her tight. He didn't know exactly what Harvey had said, but he guessed he'd implied Flora wasn't good enough to help him climb the social ladder. Everyone within twenty miles knew Harvey Illingworth was on the lookout for a wife from a wealthy and titled family, or a financial backer — a business angel.

Flora was one of the best — and

gorgeous with it. True, he wouldn't want her for a life partner himself. But only because . . .

Because why?

Because he knew all about the hurt that a relationship based only on male/female attraction could bring.

And he and Flora *didn't* get on. Even after almost two decades, neither of them really understood the other. Look how she thought he'd probably agree with whatever it was Harvey Illingworth had said about her. Well, he was sure he wouldn't. But why should Flora think he would? Why should she put him in the same mould?

That hurt, and he wasn't sure he wanted to know the answers. He glanced at Flora, then looked away as their eyes met. 'I think we ought to take a break from all of this for a while.' He'd spoken mainly to stop his own thoughts, but a break seemed like a good idea. He pushed back his cuff to check the time. 'I know it seems later, and . . . ' He looked towards the carriage clock on the mantelpiece. ' . . . no matter what Flora's clock says, it's only one o'clock. I'm taking you two out for lunch. Secret engagements, tonight's party, and the near future are strictly taboo subjects for the next couple of hours. Agreed?'

He half-expected Flora to refuse his offer of lunch — and was pleasantly surprised when she didn't.

★ ★ ★

'It was a good idea of yours, suggesting we walk into town, Flora,' said Bryce as they made their way through the park and past the cricket ground where, in season, county cricket matches were played. 'This wind is really blowing my jet lag away.'

'If I'd realised it was so windy, I might have settled for going in the car. I can hardly see where I'm going.' Flora slowed down to tuck her hair inside her coat collar.

'It's cold, too,' said Val. 'I wonder if

it's going to snow?' Then, as she caught Flora's eye, they both burst into laughter.

'Where would we be without the English trait for discussing the weather?' agreed Bryce, showing for once he was on exactly the same wavelength.

It is his kind of weather, though. Flora peeped up at him through the strands of hair covering her eyes. *Even wearing smart business clothes, he's the perfect epitome of a masculine outdoor type; striding along in the face of the wind as though he's enjoying the cold, black hair blowing across his forehead. He looks alive and virile and . . .*

Her thoughts were interrupted by a lively mud-spattered puppy bounding enthusiastically towards them and its owner calling, 'Oh, please catch him.'

Smiling, and obviously unconcerned he was sure to get mud on his black designer-label overcoat, Bryce neatly fielded the puppy. Then, holding the wriggling form vertically against his chest, he lowered his head and, turning it slightly, allowed the pup to lick his neck.

Lucky puppy. Unbidden and unwanted, the words leapt into Flora's mind. She clapped one hand over her mouth. Where on earth had that come from? She hadn't actually spoken the words, had she? A furtive upward glance towards Bryce's face reassured her on that score. His attention was on the pup's owner, who'd now reached them.

'You really should keep him on a lead until he's been trained not to run off,' Bryce scolded gently.

'Oh, I will, I will. The way you caught him was so cool. Thank you so much.' The girl, around sixteen Flora guessed, held out her arms for the puppy; and with a few bats of the eyelashes for Bryce, she walked away with obvious reluctance and frequent looks back over her shoulder.

'What a hero; what a knight in shining armour. Such adoration,' murmured Flora wickedly, her brief lapse into envying the puppy all but dismissed.

'Oh yes, my brother has a certain way

with him. He's so good with animals,'
Val said just as wickedly; and this time,
Bryce joined in the laughter.

Underlying tensions relieved for a
while, the conversation became easier
as they carried on through the park.
When they decided exactly where
they'd go for their lunch, Val, who sold
antiquarian and local interest books
from her home and knew such things,
told them the history of their chosen
destination.

'The hotel occupies the site of a
house erected by the Earl of Shrews-
bury in the sixteenth century,' she said.
'Mary, Queen of Scots, whilst in the
Earl's custody, stayed in the original
house during her visits to the area to
take the waters. She's said to have
scratched a couple of lines on a pane of
glass, and that pane is now preserved in
the museum at Poole's Cavern.'

'Enough, enough,' protested Bryce. 'I
need food, not a history lesson.' And
Flora, observing the brief squeeze he
gave Val's shoulders as they walked into

the hotel, guessed his anger towards his sister had evaporated.

They ordered their drinks and asked for a menu, and then Bryce relieved Val and Flora of their coats and removed his own. As he strode away to hang up their coats, Flora noted that the same look that had been on the teenager's face earlier was echoed on every female face in the lounge bar. 'You can almost hear their hearts beating faster,' she commented to Val, rolling her eyes. But she had to admit to herself that she wasn't totally unaware of Bryce's long back, narrow hips and long legs.

'And you, of course, are utterly immune to his charms,' Val mocked. 'But I haven't forgotten the time you bought a sloppy OTT birthday card and wrote a message on it before showing it to all our friends and telling them Bryce had sent it to you.'

'I was fifteen, Val. I've moved on since then.' But Flora felt the colour rise in her cheeks again. It was obvious from his earlier taunt that Bryce hadn't

41

forgotten that card, either. Well, he wasn't likely to, was he? She'd been reading the words she'd written out loud — with one hand over her heart, for heaven's sake — ending with 'Love and a million kisses, Bryce' before she'd realised he had come into the room. But she'd managed to cope with his oblique reference to that. She just hoped he wouldn't mention the later episode, one Val knew nothing of; because if he did, she'd want to curl up and die.

'I always thought it was rather heroic of my brother not denying he'd sent the card,' said Val. 'I remember wondering at the time why he didn't.'

'He didn't need to. The expression on his face was enough. And I knew he'd remind me about it at some future date. Like he did when I, in a loopy moment, said we should go along with your plan.' A sense of relief flowed over her as she reaffirmed how impossible Bryce could be. She'd almost allowed his charisma to shadow that knowledge.

'You're not backing out?'

Flora shook her head. 'Noo-o. But neither am I looking forward to the part I'll have to play for our families this evening.'

'You'll have Bryce to help you.'

'That's very consoling — not.' If she were honest, the thought of Bryce helping her play her part was what she dreaded most of all. There'd have to be a bit of touching hands and smiling into each other's eyes, wouldn't there? Given she wasn't attracted to Bryce, that would be embarrassing.

'You might end up enjoying yourself,' Val suggested.

'Huh. And pigs might fly,' retorted Flora.

'Yes, but listen. You — '

Bryce, their drinks and the menu arrived just then, and to Flora's relief, her friend lost interest in her and concentrated on deciding what she wanted to eat. Conversation flowed easily over their excellent meal, though Flora took time out to secretly marvel at the fact she and Bryce were managing to go so long without one of their heated arguments.

They talked about Val's book business, and the forthcoming opening of Flora's third flower boutique, and Bryce told interesting and amusing anecdotes of his lecture tour on organic farming. He was determined to implement his ideas on as many of the estate farms as possible, and Flora was fascinated as she listened and asked countless questions as well. During the last part of their meal, it was as though she and Bryce were alone, and the conversation seemed to sparkle with a special closeness.

Flora was shocked to find she felt quite put out when Val spoke, dispelling that closeness to tell them that she needed time to organise things for this evening even if they didn't. She reminded them she'd have to drive Bryce home and then go to her own house a few miles away before returning to Torman Hall for her party. 'So come on, Flora,' she concluded, 'we'll go and powder our noses while Bryce pays the bill.'

'What's all this about powdering our noses?' asked Flora after following her friend into the ladies'.

'It's just . . . well, I couldn't say anything when Bryce was anywhere around, in case he joined us before I had time to finish what I want to say. But listen, Flora, I feel awful about the way I deceived you — or at least tried to deceive you. I would have told you the whole reasoning behind my idea even if Bryce hadn't sussed it out.'

'I did feel a bit hurt you hadn't told me everything.'

'I almost did. And I would have done,' Val repeated. 'You do believe me, don't you?'

''Course I do. It's okay, I forgive you.'

'I honestly was thinking of Bryce as well as myself. I wanted you to do it for him, too.'

'I *am* doing it for Bryce too,' Flora surprised herself by saying. She was standing in front of the mirror combing her hair and caught the querying expression on Val's reflected image.

Turning, she leant back against the hand basin and continued thoughtfully, 'Hearing Bryce talk about his plans for the future and the hard work they'll involve, the criticisms and stubbornness he's prepared to face and overcome . . . Well, like you, I don't think he deserves to lose his inheritance just because he's thought to be a bit of a playboy.'

Val squeezed her friend's arm. 'I think he'll give up doing anything or going anywhere that makes him seem a playboy now.'

'He'll have to. As soon as the Jilly Joy thing has died down, as soon as she's finished her stint at the local theatre, that'll be it. That's when he'll have to watch who he's seen with, because I'm not going to pretend to be secretly engaged to him forever.'

'You won't have to keep up the pretence for long, and it'll only be necessary when the family's around,' said Val. 'The joyful Jilly is going off on a European tour when the musical's UK tour finishes. Bryce told me that on the way back from the airport.'

'But then I'll have to pretend to be upset about me and Bryce breaking things off.' Flora sighed. 'Because even when Bryce and I get un-engaged, I won't be able to tell Mum it was all a sham anyway. It wouldn't be fair to split her loyalties.'

'Hmm, I see what you mean. She's worked alongside Uncle Hector for eighteen years; it would be hard for her to participate in a lie. I'm sorry, Flora — I never even spared your mother a thought. I told you earlier that your name tripped off my tongue so easily because you're my best friend. But now I've forced you into breaking trust with your mother and mine. Oh . . . ' Val gasped in dismay.

'Yes. What a complicated web we weave. You'll be lying to your mother, too. Oh, well, they'll never know we deceived them. That's some consolation, I suppose. But we'd best get a move on, Val, or my pretend secret fiancé will be coming to fetch us.'

★ ★ ★

For a while, as the three of them walked back through the park, the only sound to break the silence was the crunching of leaves underfoot. Val, observed Flora as she glanced sideways at her friend, was wearing a dreamy look, no doubt thinking about tonight's party or her wedding.

Bryce, walking at her other side, also appeared to be deep in thought. Or maybe he just couldn't think of anything to say. *It just shows how little he and I have in common,* Flora mused. *A couple of hours or so in each other's company and we've said it all. Heaven only knows how we'll manage things tonight.*

She jumped like a jack-in-the-box when Bryce touched her lightly on the shoulder. 'I've worked something out for this evening,' he said, and the deep resonant timbre of his voice made her heart beat a little faster.

No, of course it hadn't. It was just that he'd startled her. 'Let's hear it then, Frog,' she added quickly, tapping her throat when she realised how husky she'd sounded.

'If you arrive half an hour or so before Val's party's due to start, and come up to my apartment, we'll have a private celebration first,' said Bryce. 'When I get home I'll go and see Uncle Hector and then your mother, and invite them to come have a glass of champagne with us. And . . . ' He glanced across Flora to his sister. ' . . . seeing as Mother's staying on with me for a couple of days, she'll have her travel bags with her and will probably come straight up to my place when she arrives. But I'd better phone her and tell her the news, just in case she pops in to see Uncle Hector first.'

'I told you I asked Uncle Hector not

to tell her,' said Val. 'It's a good idea though,' she added quickly. 'She'd be upset if she heard about your engagement from anyone but you.'

'And while we're celebrating this fake engagement, we'll insist that, apart from our families and . . . ' Bryce's voice hardened a fraction. ' . . . Quentin's colleague, we don't want anyone else to know for a while. Hopefully,' he continued, looking at Flora and raising one hand to show crossed fingers, 'they'll understand that we feel it wouldn't be fair to butt in on Val and Quentin's special time. Once we've explained all that to them, it won't seem strange if we're not seen living in each other's pockets all the time. Do you agree, Flora?'

By now, they'd reached the grounds of the large Victorian house where Flora had her flat, and Bryce had leant nonchalantly against his sister's parked car to put that question. Flora thought she detected a cool challenge in his gaze, and for some reason that bugged her. It had to be the challenging look that had got under her skin; she certainly didn't want to 'live in his pocket', did she?

'Oh, yes, I agree,' she told him. 'And it'll be the best of both worlds for you, Bryce. You'll be able to pay attention to your countless girlfriends and not worry about upsetting your uncle because he'll think you're safely engaged. You can have your cake and eat it as well.'

'So can you,' he drawled. 'What's good for the gander — '

'This goose doesn't happen to want cake.' She'd snapped the retort, realising bitterly that she and Bryce were back to their normal selves.

Bryce obviously realised it too; after manoeuvring himself into Val's car — Val was already in the driving seat tapping her fingers against the wheel — he pulled the door shut and gave a mocking wave.

When she got indoors, Flora poured a glass of elderflower cordial and took it into the living room. She snuggled down on the sofa and stared into the gently glowing fire.

What on earth had possessed her to make that comment about countless girlfriends? It had made her sound as though she was jealous, when in reality she couldn't care less how many girlfriends Bryce had. After all, he'd long ago let her know she wasn't a suitable type for him.

Heck, she didn't want to remember that time; she really, really didn't. But unwillingly she did — and it felt as though it were happening here and now . . .

★   ★   ★

It was a beautiful May evening. Pink flowery spires stood proud on the horse-chestnut trees, the laburnum rained gold on the cottage garden, and the scent of lilac and hawthorn mingled in the warm air. She was wearing brief shorts and a T-shirt that was last year's, raked out because of the unexpected warm weather — a bit past its wear-by date, really; but that didn't matter, as she wouldn't be seeing anyone. Val had told her that the whole Torman family was going to the opera.

Her hair was caught up in a ponytail, her feet were bare, and she delighted in the touch of the grass as she dawdled through the buttercup meadow which tomorrow would house the marquee and bandstand in honour of the May Festival that was held on the grounds every year.

She and Val always added to the fun by hiding a present for each other. This time she was going to hide it in the hayloft above the old barn. There was a gap in between the rafters and the hayloft roof that she'd be able to reach by standing on one of the old wooden barrels.

When she reached the barn, the farmyard cat was sitting near the top of the rickety ladder that led to the hayloft, wagging his tail and staring upwards. 'Oh no,' she gasped, following the cat's steady gaze, 'the swallows are nesting in the apex. You are not going to get the baby birds, puss.'

She threw the parcel down behind her onto a pile of hay, and then climbed up to get the cat. 'There. Got you.' It struggled and wriggled in her arms; she lost her balance and felt herself falling.

Everything was slightly hazy. The cat had got away and she found herself lying in the hay on top of Bryce. Slowly she wriggled to a sitting position, and, looking down at him, said stupidly, 'You're supposed to be at the opera.'

'No 'thank you for breaking my fall, Bryce'; just 'you're supposed to be at the opera',' he said mockingly.

'Well, you *are* supposed to be at the opera.'

'Unfortunately, a sick cow over at Manifold Farm prevented me from going.'

'Oh, I see. Anyway, would you mind moving, Bryce? I think you're lying on Val's present.' She was on her knees now, feeling around in the hay for the parcel. She caught a glimpse of red and gold wrapping paper beneath Bryce's head and stretched over his prone body to tug at the parcel.

'Ask me properly and I'll move,' he drawled.

At almost sixteen, teetering on the brink of young adulthood, her hormones kicked in violently. His voice did something to her, and she recalled the words she'd written on that birthday card last year when she'd pretended he'd signed it with love and a million kisses. Suddenly she was finding it hard to breathe. She could smell the warmth of him mingling with the sweet smell of the hay; could feel his breath on her neck.

'You mean you want me to kiss you?' she whispered.

'No. I didn't mean — '

But she traced his lips with her fingers and then lowered her face so her lips could touch his.

For a nanosecond, she was sure he'd started to kiss her back. But then he moved violently away from her. Sitting up now, his hands clasped around his knees, he took several deep breaths then said harshly, 'For heaven's sake, Flora, can't you see that . . . anything . . . any kind of relationship between us wouldn't be right? I'm — '

'You're the great Bryce Torman.' Hurt transmuted into anger and she leapt to her feet. 'You think anyone and everyone wants to be kissed by you. Well, I don't. I don't want you ever to come near me again. You're just a despicable, arrogant being. Do you hear me, Bryce *Torment*?'

* * *

She hadn't waited to see if he'd replied, Flora recalled now, sipping at her cordial. She'd run home and gone straight to bed. She'd cried herself to sleep and had woken next morning knowing she despised Bryce; knowing she would despise him forever, because the unfortunate episode had brought grim acceptance.

56

Of course any relationship between the future heir to the Torman Empire and the daughter of an estate worker wouldn't be right, but Bryce needn't have pointed it out so cruelly.

Over the years her violent dislike of him had dwindled, and in adulthood she learned to cope with the hurt he'd caused her by engineering arguments whenever they were obliged to be in each other's company. Just like she had as a little girl, really, before the episode in the barn. Though these days it wasn't for childish fun but to help her sustain an enforced immunity to him.

And now ... Now that immunity was going to be sorely tried. 'How ironic,' she muttered aloud, 'that I've agreed to play the part of his fiancée.'

But like Val had said — even though it was a mock engagement — it was a shame they were keeping it secret from everyone except family and Quentin's colleague. It would have been good to see Harvey's reaction; his attitude towards relationships was similar to Bryce's.

Unlike Bryce, Harvey hadn't been born into the 'upper echelon', but he was determined to get there by marriage. Which meant Flora wasn't good enough for him.

Oh, well, she and Harvey were history; from now on there'd be no room for anything in her life except her career. Playing the part of Bryce's fiancée when the odd occasion demanded it would just be an amusing interlude. And, she realised, it was more than time she started to get ready for the first of the amusing interludes.

4

Dark clouds gloomed in the night sky; no moon and only the odd defiant star dotted the heavy blanket above. A ponderous sort of evening, thought Flora as she locked her car.

Feeling slightly nervous, she glanced upwards at Bryce's part of the Hall. Even the redolence of woodsmoke in the air and the soft glow from behind closed curtains, which at any other time would have seemed welcoming, failed to lift her mood. Bryce's self-contained wing was in the upper two storeys at the back and, she realised now, she'd never even seen it. The rest of the Hall she knew as well as she did her own home.

Breathing deeply to try and quell her nerves, and telling herself it was ridiculous to feel like this anyway, she mounted the flight of stone steps which led up to the front door. She rang the bell and was dismayed when the door opened so quickly. 'Here you are, sweetheart.' Bryce's eyes sparkled with merriment and he'd spoken louder than was necessary — which must mean someone was already here. 'I'll have to find you a door key,' he continued, drawing her inside. 'My fiancée shouldn't have to ring the bell. Let me take your coat. But first . . . '

His face full of mischief, he pulled her into his arms. His mouth found hers with unerring instinct — gentle and caressing and . . . and . . .

Heavenly, thought Flora, totally unable to prevent her lips from parting slightly and responding to the warmth of his kiss. To her dismay, she felt her hands sneaking up his shirt front. It was a blue silk shirt — she'd noticed that the second he'd opened the door; noticed he wasn't wearing a jacket; noted too, that his shirt was open at his throat, revealing a tantalising glimpse of dark hairs.

It was here her hands came to rest, the wiriness of those dark hairs slightly abrasive under her fingers. Fingers that suddenly took on a life of their own, lingering for a moment to glory in the beating of the pulse in the hollow of his throat, then tracing a delicate path up his neck, over his chin, along his jaw bone; another pulse — surely beating faster? just beneath his ear, then the silkiness of his shirt collar at the back of his neck. Wiry hair again, the back of his head warm and slightly damp as though he'd recently had a shower.

Yes, the scent of his cologne tantalised her, and she could taste a hint of spearmint on his lips. But then he lifted his head, stepped back slightly and removed her coat all in one lithe movement, and she felt bereft before indignation came to her rescue.

'There was no need for that, Bryce. They can't see into the hall.'

'Who can't?' His face was alight with fiendish glee as he stood holding her coat, looking down at her. 'Who can't?' he asked again.

'You wouldn't . . . you didn't . . . ?'

She didn't have to push him out of her way; he stepped aside, hanging her coat on an oak hall robe, and allowed her to stalk past him and to go through the open door which obviously led to the living room.

It was, as she'd suddenly suspected, devoid of any people. Bryce had tricked her. And so had her darned hormones. They'd no right to go zinging out of control like that, as if she'd never been kissed before. But no other kiss had made her bones dissolve and her limbs tremble like that one had.

And, she realised with horror as her mind played a lightning retake of Bryce's kiss, her hormones were still at it. Confused thoughts and feelings tumbled through her mind and she wanted — needed — time to pull herself together.

But it was too late. A prickling at the back of her neck alerted Flora to the fact Bryce was standing behind her. She took a deep breath, silently counting up to ten. She'd only reached three when she heard first a snigger — no other word for that sound — then a chuckle, and then his deep hearty laughter filled the room.

* * *

Flora whirled round to face Bryce, her eyes sparkling with temper. 'You're nothing but a . . . Oh, I can't think of a word to describe what you are. You made me think someone was here.'

'I didn't say so, Flora. You drew your own conclusions.'

'Yes, because you spoke so loudly, and then — '

'And then I kissed you. And you kissed me back. And quite enjoyable it was, too.'

He wished he couldn't remember quite so vividly how enjoyable he'd found that kiss. He'd been unable to resist making her think that somebody was already here. And he'd known how she'd react when she found out what he'd done. He'd always been able to spark her into indignation or temper.

Most of the time, when she was younger — when the age gap between them had made him see her only as his kid sister's best friend, teasing her into a childish tantrum had amused him. Until that May evening in the barn when he'd suddenly realised she was growing up. He hadn't found that at all funny.

And now, this evening, he'd only meant to brush her lips before telling her nobody else had arrived yet. But she'd looked so appealing, all wide-eyed and breathless, her honey-gold hair in a sort of topknot high on her head, lending an extra inch or so to her five-foot-two height.

He hadn't meant it to turn into a real kiss. He didn't want there to be anything between him and Flora; his idea of a relationship wasn't of one where half the time would be spent bickering with each other. He'd been there, done that. But when Flora's lips had parted under his, when her hands had started to wander over his chest, up to his throat, around his neck . . .

The ringing of the doorbell put a brake on his thoughts, and he felt more than a little thankful. He glanced at Flora; her cheeks were pink and her eyes were sparkling. Okay, he knew that was because she was mad at him. But her mouth . . . well, that still showed signs of having been kissed. And he told her so, before walking away to go and open the front door.

For a second, Flora was tempted to call the whole thing off. She couldn't cope with this, didn't want to cope with it. Bryce had had no right to kiss her like that, forcing his way through the barriers she'd built to protect herself from him; trying to break down the secure wall of her aversion towards him.

But Val's happiness is at stake, she reminded herself. *I've got to go through with it. I'll just have to make sure there's no repeat performance of what happened when I arrived.*

From the hall she could hear Bryce's

voice, relaxed and warm, mingling with his mother's voice. Then Mrs Torman hurried into the room. Widowed five years previously, she was plump, tiny, and moved in a bird-like way. Tonight she looked just like a jolly robin, Flora thought, going forward to greet her and finding herself enfolded in a warm embrace.

'Bryce is just putting my travel bags in the guest room,' she said. 'Flora, my dear, I was so happy when he phoned to tell me the news. And — ' A cloud touched the twinkling eyes for a moment. ' — his father would have been delighted, too. He always had a soft spot for you. Used to admire you for standing no nonsense from this son of mine. Ah, what a happy Christmas it's going to be. As soon as Val and Quentin are married you must announce your engagement properly.'

Mrs Torman stepped back and, smiling, she nodded her head. 'From the way you look, you won't be able to keep your secret long, anyway. It will be obvious to everyone that you're a woman in love.'

Bryce walked in just in time to hear his mother's remark. 'I made a similar comment just before I let you in,' he said outrageously.

'So tell me, Flora,' said Mrs Torman, 'when did he come to his senses and realise he was in love with you?'

Oh, no. They should have realised one of their mothers would want to hear details. Why hadn't they worked out answers for that sort of question? Flora sneaked a look at Bryce and thought she detected panic in his eyes. Aha. Payback time for that kiss. 'Do tell her, Bryce,' she said, struggling to keep a straight face. 'It was so romantic.'

There was a tiny silence, then Bryce chuckled, and Flora just knew she shouldn't have challenged him. 'Val asked me to pick up something she'd left at Flora's flat,' he said. 'There was no reply when I knocked on the door, but Val had given me the key in case Flora was out, and I let myself in.'

He stepped closer to Flora and put his arm around her shoulders. 'I discovered Flora was at home after all,' he continued. 'She was in that huge air bath of hers. That's why she hadn't heard me knock on the door. Anyway . . . ' He feathered a finger down Flora's cheek. ' . . . I offered to get — '

Flora felt a wave of colour sweep up her face. 'Bryce, stop it.' To her dismay her voice was husky. Temper, that's what it was. Nothing to do with the way her cheek was tingling under his finger.

'Stop this . . . ' His finger circled her cheek again. ' . . . or stop telling Mother — '

'Don't tease her, Bryce.' His mother laughed. 'You needn't tell me any more. I might be past my first youth, but I can imagine the rest for myself.'

To Flora's relief, Bryce stepped away from her and gave his mother a quick hug. 'Come and sit down,' he said. 'You, too, Flora; then you can chat in comfort.'

'Chat to my future daughter-in-law,' Mrs Torman chirped happily, allowing Bryce to guide her to the deep leather armchair in front of the blazing log fire.

'You must both come and stay with me for a couple of days after Val's wedding, Flora. You've never seen my little house and you'll love the part of Cheshire I live in, though the country-side's a lot gentler than that near your Macclesfield shop, and than Derbyshire of course. You will come, won't you?'

'We'll spend New Year's with you if you like, Mother.' Bryce bent down to add another log to the fire, then glanced towards her, his assured smile encompassing Flora, who was sitting on the arm of his mother's chair. 'We haven't made any other arrangements.'

Flora glared at him. 'Surely you haven't forgotten,' she replied mock-sweetly, 'that I'll be away for New Year's.'

Then, hiding her anger, she looked down at Mrs Torman. 'I'm doing the flowers for a New Year's Ball in London. It's a joint effort with Tilly, my partner in the London business. It'll be a huge do; the client's a well-known actor. There'll be photographers from an upmarket glossy magazine, and that will be good publicity. Tilly and I have been invited to stay over for the night.'

It was partly true, Flora defended silently. She had been invited to stay on as a guest, and had firmly but politely declined. But Bryce wasn't to know that, and she'd no intention of allowing him to plan her life. Besides, she felt guilty enough already about deceiving his mother, and that deceit would seem even worse if she actually stayed in Mrs Torman's home.

Bryce's teasing, smiling look changed to one of grim determination. Flora knew he was about to make some kind of stand. After all, wouldn't that be expected of him as her fiancé?

The ringing of the doorbell broke into what could have become a heated moment between them. Though it wasn't much consolation, for now her own mother and Bryce's uncle had arrived, and she was going to have to cope with their congratulations and

70

suffer a champagne toast to herself and Bryce.

★ ★ ★

Twenty minutes later, Flora's jaws ached from smiling and her body was stiff. She'd tensed herself every time Bryce touched her; had bitten into her lip when he'd replied to his uncle's toast by kissing her.

And now they were on their way down to the main part of the building for Val's party, and she'd have to continue her act a good while longer for the benefit of Quentin, his business colleague and Val and Bryce's cousin Rupert — the one who'd gain if Bryce was disinherited. She should be able to see the funny side of it, really. Trying to behave as if she welcomed Bryce's 'pretend' loving touches for their audience; trying to behave as if she didn't for her own sake.

No-oo. She didn't welcome his touches. Of course she didn't.

'We're doing well, Flora,' Bryce whispered as they walked through Torman Hall's front door. 'You're making a great job of being my fiancée.'

His breath was warm in her ear and his lips lightly grazed her earlobe — one of her most sensitive spots, and she couldn't control the tiny gasp that escaped. Because he'd tickled her. That was all.

Surely Bryce couldn't be thinking differently, she thought as he gave a low, husky laugh. Drat the man; she'd have to do something to show him his make-believe touches weren't having any effect on her.

Well, okay, she'd circulate and chat, behave in a bright and breezy manner and let him see that none of this had affected her in the slightest. She was feeling at odds with herself because they were deceiving their mothers and Bryce's uncle and not because whenever Bryce came near her, she kept recalling that stupid moment in the hall when she'd enjoyed being in his arms.

Thought I'd enjoyed being in his arms, she corrected hastily. That was just a blip. Even though it was a pretty big one; that's all it had been.

* * *

Time passed quicker than Flora expected it to. Val had persuaded Bryce to go and fetch his fiddle. Flora smiled as she watched him play. She'd been about ten when, just to annoy him, she'd called his expensive *Georges Chanot* violin a fiddle, and the term had stuck.

It was a few years since she'd heard his repertoire of classical, folk and jig music, and she'd forgotten how good he was. But when he played 'The Floral Dance' for her — well, to annoy her, she felt sure — without thinking, she stuck out her tongue. Bryce faltered and played a few wrong notes, and Val made a cheeky comment about Flora teasing him. Although she wanted the floor to open up and swallow her, Flora managed to join in the laughter.

Bryce finished off with 'Chapel of Love' for Val and Quentin, and Flora had to blink away a tear. Not because she wished that song were for her, she told herself. It was a tear of happiness for her best friend.

The music over, everyone made their way to the buffet table. The food was delicious; Flora found herself next to Quentin's business colleague, Yasem, who was charming and seemed genuinely interested in hearing about her flower boutiques. After a while, Bryce's cousin Rupert took Yasem's place and made her laugh with hilarious tales of life as an antique dealer.

But all the time, Flora was aware of Bryce's gaze on her. And eventually, when their eyes met across the room, she was puzzled by the expression she thought she read in his. Perhaps he was just impatient to end the evening. Well, she had a good enough excuse for being the first to leave. She'd got an early start in the morning.

She walked across the room to Bryce

74

and then, together, they made their farewells. But Val's whispered, 'Big brother looks mad enough to eat you alive,' as she kissed Flora goodbye, confirmed Flora's original thought.

Bryce was angry. But why? She hadn't done anything to cause it. Had she?

* * *

Although curious as to what might have caused Bryce's anger, there was no way she was going to ask him, thought Flora, turning on the bottom step to wave to Val and Quentin in the doorway.

Nor was she going to try and match his long strides as he made his way with break-neck speed over the gravelled driveway that fronted Torman Hall. No. She was only hurrying because it was cold. Only asking, 'So, what's rattled your cage?' because she couldn't bear the foreboding atmosphere that surrounded him like a cloak.

His head jerked sideways. 'Don't pretend you don't know, Flora.'

She hadn't the faintest idea; but even though she felt she had a volcano ready to erupt at her side, at least he'd slowed down slightly. Maybe because he was hoping for some response. But what did he expect her to say? Okay, it had been a long, tough day to say the least. And, after the stunt Bryce had pulled when she'd arrived this evening — then the way he'd answered his mother's question, if anyone had the right to be angry, it certainly wasn't him. But she'd managed to push both incidents to the back of her mind, and she felt quite pleased with the way she'd acted her part.

Nobody had questioned the reason they'd given for keeping the engagement a secret. The *fake* engagement secret. Though Rupert had managed to flirt and sympathise at the same time: 'If you were my fiancée, I'd want to tell the world. Immediately.' That's what he'd said.

Recalling his words, and imagining Bryce wanting to do such a thing, Flora chuckled aloud.

'It wasn't funny, Flora.' Bryce's words sounded colder than the touch of the icy wind that greeted them as they turned onto the path that led to the small court-yard at the back of the building.

'What wasn't?' Flora glanced upwards and wondered if it was the pale bluish glow from the old-fashioned lamp-posts dotted around the courtyard giving Bryce's face such a harsh look.

'The way you let Yasem monopolise you for over an hour was bad enough. Though I can see that you had to be polite to Quentin's important guest. No doubt Val and Quentin are very grateful to you. But there was no need for you to spend the rest of your time with Rupert. I'm sure my mother and Uncle Hector wondered what you were playing at. After all, they think we're engaged, yet you were so obviously enjoying my cousin's attentions.'

He paused as if waiting for some

comment. Flora rolled her lips inwards and bit down on them.

'I'm surprised you couldn't see through his false charm,' Bryce added. 'My cousin Rupert can't help but flirt with anything wearing a skirt.'

Talk about the pot calling the kettle black. Flora's fingers curled into her palms inside her coat pockets. She breathed deeply. Her breath, exhaled through her nose, lingered on the cold air. Of course she'd seen through Rupert; and for that very reason, she'd found his attentions funny and amusing, and had enjoyed flirting harmlessly in return. But there was no need for Bryce to speak to her in such a derogatory manner; she strongly objected to being called something wearing a skirt. Yes. And Bryce knew she'd object to that. She dug her nails harder into her palms. She wouldn't give him the satisfaction of a reply. They were only a few yards from her car now. Inside her head, she counted each step she took. Nearly there.

'I imagine he offered to show you round his showroom? That's his equivalent of 'Would you like to see my etchings?' If you know what's good for you, you'll stay away from him.'

She couldn't take that in silence. 'Is that an order, Bryce? It rather sounded like one.'

'Believe it or not, I wouldn't like you to get hurt.' Flora was quite touched by his reply. Until he added, 'But, yes, I'd like you to stay away from Rupert, because if you were seen with him and the family got to hear of it, I can't imagine what they'd think.'

'They'll think I'm being friendly towards my future cousin-in-law, who I happen to like quite a lot. And talking about think . . . ' She pulled her hands out of her pockets, unzipped her shoulder-bag and reached inside it for her car keys. 'The family may think we're secretly engaged, but we know we're not,' she continued. 'Besides, what was it you said about how things would progress after we'd told them the reason for the secrecy? 'It won't seem strange if we're not seen to live in each other's pockets all the time'.'

'And what was your reply?' Bryce covered her hand with his as she started to open her car door. 'Something about not wanting cake. Well, from the way you were flirting with Rupert, it looked like you were more than willing to accept crumbs from his table.'

'I told you. I like him.' She did, but she'd never want anything other than friendship from him; and in spite of his flirtatious manner towards her, she knew Rupert didn't fancy her.

Bryce's grip on her hand tightened fractionally. 'If I didn't know better,' muttered Flora, managing to pull her hand from under his and turning to face him, 'I'd think you were jealous.'

She expected him to laugh or come out with some mocking response. Instead, he studied her face for endless seconds as though surprised at what he was seeing. And when his eyes lingered on her mouth, Flora felt a sharp current shoot through her body. She just knew he was going to kiss her. Well, she wouldn't let him.

But when he lowered his head, she felt frozen to the spot — powerless to turn her face away. For the briefest of moments, his mouth on hers was hard, almost angry. Then it gentled and she felt the whisper of little ghost kisses; one second warm and soft, and then . . . tingly as his evening shadow beard grazed her delicate skin.

She knew she should pull away. She meant to pull away. So why were her arms pulling him closer? The myriad kisses deepened into one; her lips parted on a sigh and obeyed the silent demands of his without question. It was a repeat — no, it was a continuation of the kiss in his hallway.

He controlled her mouth as he had the fiddle, bringing it to life under his touch, fine-tuning the dance of his tongue with hers; slow at first as it stroked and teased, tantalising feather touches on sensitive places, making her wait with quivering delight for more. She was entirely caught up in her own emotions, totally entranced by the magic of his mouth. Then, with a suddenness that shocked her, he lifted his head and stepped back.

And, through her shock, she realised what she'd done. Not only had she allowed his intimate exploration of her mouth, but she'd actually encouraged it. The thought was pathetic. Unbearable. This was Bryce Torman, for heaven's sake, and she'd sworn long ago never to give him the power to hurt her again. No way must he suspect what his kiss had made her feel — made her yearn for.

Drawing on resources she wasn't aware she possessed, she forced herself to look him in the eye and said, 'Now I know why I favour crumbs.' But even before she uttered the words, she was aware that the gloating look she'd expected to see on Bryce's face wasn't there. He looked . . . bewildered? Stunned?

The static in the blue luminescence

surrounding them was almost tangible. His gaze rooted her to the spot and with every breath she took, she was ridiculously aware of the fragrance from winter flowering honeysuckle and witch hazel. Or maybe she was concentrating on the aroma to try and alleviate the feel of his kiss, which was still on her lips.

Time became meaningless. It could have been seconds, it could have been hours. Just as Flora was wondering how much longer she'd feel powerless to move, Bryce murmured something like 'Drive safely' before he turned and walked away.

* * *

He couldn't believe what he'd done. It had been different earlier, when he'd engineered the kiss in the hallway. That, although it had somehow turned into a proper kiss, had been to tease her, to annoy her even. It had just been a bit of fun.

This time, though he couldn't work out why, for one crazy second an unfamiliar feeling had overtaken him and he'd wanted to crush her lips against his own. But that feeling of . . . of whatever it had been . . . hadn't lasted longer than a blink of an eye. And that was when he should have stopped. But he hadn't, had he? His mouth had taken on a mind of its own and he'd been lost in the dreamy deliciousness of her soft velvety skin, her light floral perfume; of holding her in his arms.

He'd wanted more. But she was his sister's best friend, and her mother and his uncle worked together — a brief fling with Flora was out of the question. Because anything between them would be brief. Passion would die quickly, and they'd end up at each other's throats as usual. Even a fighting friendship between them after any kind of fling would be impossible. And that would affect the friendships between his family and hers. Besides, he unwillingly admitted with what felt like a pang of hurt, Flora had made it obvious that his kiss had done nothing at all for her.

Why on earth had he agreed to this fake secret engagement? he wondered as he let himself in and strode quickly into the living room to pour a much-needed drink. Quentin wouldn't have let Val go; wouldn't have accepted her reason for calling the wedding off. And if Uncle Hector disinherited him . . . well, it would hurt to lose Torman Hall and the farming estates, but he'd survive.

Everything had happened too quickly. He'd been tired after his lecture tour, unable to think clearly when Val had sprung his fake secret engagement to Flora on him. Okay, he'd refused to go along with it at first; but then he'd let Flora, with her talk of Val's happiness and his brotherly feeling, sway him.

He finished his drink in one gulp and banged his glass down. He was still too tired to think straight. He'd sleep on it, and maybe tomorrow he'd come up with a way to get out of this mess.

Maybe tomorrow he'd see Flora as the aggravating, impossible person she was. And if Rupert wanted to start seeing Flora, well . . . so be it.

But it wasn't the aggravating, impossible Flora he dreamed about when he finally drifted into sleep. It was the Flora who'd responded to his kiss, the Flora who'd pulled him closer, the Flora who made him wish the engagement was for real.

★ ★ ★

When he woke, his sensible side took over. Even if Flora was attracted to him — and she wasn't — there could never be anything between them. He'd learned the hard way about a relationship based on arguments and attraction and nothing else. True, that had been years ago, he'd been far away from home in Australia, and when he'd lost the one special friend he'd made to an older and richer rival, he'd been young enough to imagine his heart had been broken. It hadn't of course, but he still remembered the hurt.

As for Flora . . . well, he had enjoyed telling her his plans and ideas for organic farming, and she'd seemed genuinely interested. Maybe, even though there couldn't be anything else, they could become friends? It would be good to have someone to talk to, to share ideas with. Perhaps she'd agree to come for another lunch today? Just the two of them this time. It was still early; he'd call in at her Buxton shop and see if he could catch her there when she came back from the flower market.

But when he arrived at Daisy Chain, to his dismay Rupert was there. And that unfamiliar feeling he couldn't place sneaked up on him again.

5

Flora, her arms full of boxes, pushed open the door with her bottom. 'It's me, Sue,' she called over the tinkling of the shop bell. 'Talk about stating the obvious,' she added as the attractive redhead who managed this flower boutique for her — the second in her Daisy Chain — came out of the preparation room. 'I mean, it's hardly likely to be anyone else this early in the morning.'

'That's what you think. You've already had two visitors.'

Flora noted that Sue looked slightly flustered as she moved forward to relieve her of the boxes of flowers. 'It's not eight o'clock yet. Surely it wasn't sales reps?' said Flora, moving towards the door. Unloading time was limited; she didn't want a parking ticket.

'No.' Sue placed the boxes carefully

on the counter, then followed Flora back out to her Range Rover. 'The first was Rupert Torman-White. He asked me to remind you about your lunch date with him.'

'The other was . . . ?' Flora prompted as she reached into the back of the vehicle for some more boxes.

'Was . . . er . . . was Mr Torman. Mr Bryce Torman. He arrived while the first one, Rupert Torman-White, was giving me the message for you.'

Sue seemed embarrassed now, and Flora wondered which of the two visitors her manageress had felt attracted to, for she could see no other reason for her attitude. They were both perfectly capable of upstaging Casanova, Rupert so blond and Bryce so dark. And either one of them could have flirted with Sue. Though why that should have affected her was hard to say; Sue could win a gold when it came to flirting back.

However, as Sue stood, her arms full of boxes, making no attempt to carry them into the shop, the reason for her embarrassment became clear. 'He . . . er . . . that is, Mr Bryce Torman told Mr Torman-White you wouldn't be available for lunch as you had a prior engagement with him. Said perhaps I'd kindly remind you of that — and to tell you he'd pick you up at your flat at twelve-thirty so . . . so please make sure you're there.' The last bit of the message came out in a rush.

'Thanks, Sue. Now, let's get these boxes in before I get a parking ticket.' Flora gave Sue a reassuring smile, but inside she was seething. Bryce's choice of words wasn't lost on her. He was reminding her of their supposed secret engagement just as he had last night when he'd told her to stay away from his cousin Rupert.

Even though he'd said he'd *like* her to stay away, he'd been *telling* her to, really. Not that she'd mentioned she'd arranged to go to Rupert's showrooms. She hadn't got round to that. Because . . .

Because she'd allowed herself to get lost in Bryce's kiss; and then, when she'd come out with that derogatory comment, there'd been that strange interlude when she'd been powerless to look away from him. It had taken ages for her to gather enough strength to get into the car and drive home once he'd walked away.

Even after she'd had a shower and drunk a mug of hot chocolate, the taste and memory of Bryce's kiss had still lingered. Had still lingered, too, when she'd lain in her comfortable bed with its attractive bedding, extravagant linen and lace confections scattered with blue, rose and green flowers, which usually had the power to soothe and relax her. She'd been unable to work out why Bryce wanted her to stay away from Rupert. She'd even wondered, for a lunatic second, if Bryce had kissed her because her remark about liking his cousin a lot had made him jealous.

Now, as she helped Sue sort the flowers, she realised she'd probably dented Bryce's pride, damaged his ego, by spending more time at the party with Rupert than with him. If that was the case, she must have done more than damage Bryce's ego with the comment she'd made.

Well, tough. None of that gave him any right to cancel her arrangement for lunch. She'd phone Rupert later, and if he wanted to see her some other time, she'd go. Besides, she wanted to look round his showrooms; from what he'd told her last night, it sounded as though several of his antique urns would be useful to her. She wanted something different and unusual for her flower arrangements at the charity auction that was being held in a couple of weeks. As for today, if Bryce really thought she'd be at her flat at twelve-thirty, he'd got another think coming.

When she arrived at her Macclesfield shop which, when her new premises were ready, she'd be leaving in the care of Justin, her trainee manager, Flora made up huge vases of flowers for delivery to three upmarket restaurants. Then she phoned Val and asked her if she'd a couple of hours to spare. 'I thought we could go and look round the church and make the final decision on the flowers for your wedding.' For, as well as being chief bridesmaid to her friend, Flora was also decorating the beautiful village church where Val was to be married.

Flora spent longer than she'd meant to with Val because they called in at an art and craft centre that had recently opened in a refurbished mill. She had her 'business only' mobile phone with her; she knew Justin or Sue could contact her if there were any queries or problems.

Apart from both shops delivering fresh flower arrangements to the restaurants, hotels and business premises that had a weekly standing order, Mondays were quiet and there wouldn't be any speciality blooms arriving from abroad.

By the time they'd finished looking around, and Flora had bought a few interesting bits and pieces she thought would be useful for theme parties, it was four-thirty, so she decided to take the rest of the afternoon off and went home.

She hadn't been in long when Mrs Torman phoned. 'I hoped you might be in, seeing as you weren't at either shop. I tried your mobile but it was switched off.'

'I don't use my personal mobile during the day,' said Flora. 'Just my business one, and only the shop staff have that number.'

'Very sensible,' said Mrs Torman. 'Now, how about taking pity on me tonight and coming for a meal at that hotel where Bakewell pudding was invented?'

'Taking pity on you?'

'Yes. Today is the first Monday in the month. You know what that means.'

'Oh, of course. Tenants' meeting, held over supper and drinks.' Flora relaxed. Bryce would be presiding over that meeting as he always did. There was no chance of him turning up with his mother. 'I'd love to come for a meal.

Shall I pick you up?'

'No, don't worry, dear. I'll make my own way there. See you about eight o'clock?'

And Flora agreed, though she was worried that Mrs Torman might ask questions which would be hard to answer. This travesty of being secretly engaged to Bryce looked like becoming more complicated than she'd ever thought.

★   ★   ★

It was a few minutes before eight when Flora drove in to the well-lit carpark of one of the county's best known hotels — the successor of an eighteenth century posting house demolished and rebuilt by the fifth Duke of Rutland. The number of cars parked, so early in the week, spoke for the hotel's popularity; it was in fact popular with celebrities from far and wide.

Mrs Torman is already here, Flora observed with a smile as she recognised the small bright green Healey Frog-Eyed Sprite that Bryce's mother had driven for years. 'Froggie' was a much-cherished member of the family; nothing could persuade Mrs Torman to buy a car more suitable for someone of her age.

There's a strong streak of stubbornness in the Tormans, mused Flora as she made her way inside. *Mrs Torman, Hector, Val, Bryce — they've all got it.*

This affirmation was proved dramatically and unexpectedly when after feeling a gentle tap on her shoulder, Flora turned, a ready smile on her lips for Mrs Torman, and found herself looking up at Bryce. 'You're supposed to be at the tenants' meeting,' she said, then bit her lip as a spectre of the past rose up to tantalise her. How similar this evening's words were to those long-ago words, 'You're supposed to be at the opera.'

Bryce obviously remembered too, for he drawled, 'No sick cow tonight, but a couple of sick farmers. The monthly meeting has been postponed until next week.'

And you were so determined to get your own way about seeing me today that you used the situation to those ends, Flora responded silently while forcing herself to show nothing other than a bland expression, managing to look coolly up at him.

He continued, 'We've time for a drink before our meal; the table's booked for eight-thirty.' He sounded confident enough, but there was a wary look in his eyes.

He isn't quite sure how I'm going to react to his trickery in getting me here, guessed Flora. She wasn't quite sure herself, but after a moment's pause she decided to give in gracefully. 'Mineral water for me, please.' Trying to ignore the gleam of satisfaction that replaced the wary look, she sauntered to an unoccupied table.

However satisfied he looked, he was half expecting me to walk out, she thought. *Really, for once, I've got the*

*upper hand. He'll be wondering all
evening whether I'm going to challenge
him. Well, I'll keep him wondering.*

She curved her lips into a smile as he
walked towards her with their drinks
and tried to drown out the 'tall, dark
and to die for' refrain that kept
repeating itself in the uncontrollable
part of her mind. But he looked so
stunning in the superbly cut light grey
suit, teamed with a black shirt — which
just had to be silk — and a tie of a
psychedelic design. Then she smothered
a giggle as she pictured him behind the
wheel of Froggie. True, it was a classic
car, and therefore had a certain
prestige, but it was a far cry from his
sleek Ferrari or even his Range Rover.

*How he must have hated his journey
here. And he's got to drive home in
discomfort as well*, she thought glee-
fully.

'Private joke, or can anyone join in?'
he queried as he slid onto the wooden
settle opposite her.

'Oh, very private.' She chuckled

provocatively, deliberately setting out to cause bewilderment by her carefree mood.

A silence fell between them, and she sipped her drink between glancing casually round the other tables. She was determined that Bryce would be the one to break the silence. Unfortunately, he seemed just as determined not to, and time seemed to lengthen into eternity. *Oh yes, he's stubborn all right*, thought Flora. She glanced at him from beneath her eyelashes. His chiselled jaw was set in hard lines, but she detected a slight twitching of his lips. Involuntarily, her eyes flew open and she accidentally met his.

That was her undoing, as her laughter welled up and escaped. A laughter in which Bryce joined wholeheartedly. Flora became aware of her heart beating faster as she sensed a primeval recognition between them.

Oh no she did *not*. Thanks to him, she hadn't had any lunch. The coffee and cream cake she'd had at the arts and crafts centre didn't count, she told herself. What she felt now was hunger. And keeping this thought uppermost, she said, 'At least I'll get a good meal out of it.'

'So you will.' He glanced down at his watch, but not before Flora had perceived his eyes glittering like dark turbulent pools in a storm, though they were blank when he lifted them to state, 'And it's time to move over to the restaurant.'

She was fully aware of the sly looks they received; she knew exactly what people, especially the women, were thinking as they walked through to the restaurant, Bryce's hand lightly beneath her elbow. They'd got her down as one of Bryce's playthings, for his face and reputation were well-known throughout the county. 'I don't know whether they're envying me or pitying me,' she muttered.

If Bryce heard, he refrained from comment. He did, however, once they were settled in their place, comment wickedly on her heightened colour. 'You look like one of your pretty pink roses,' he teased, 'or maybe like peaches and cream.' This time *she* chose to ignore *his* words, turning her eyes instead to the menu handed to her.

'Whatever is Herdwick Macon?' she wondered aloud.

'Slices of smoked mutton served with pears and mint,' Bryce informed her. 'It used to be a traditional speciality in Derbyshire, so it's good to see it on the menu again. I don't think I'll have it this evening. You should try it, though. It's delicious.'

'Maybe, but it might be one of the estate's sheep. It might be one I stroked, or even one I helped bottle-feed as a lamb. I think I'll have the sautéed tiger prawns.'

'You'd never make a farmer's wife,' he said lightly; and Flora was amazed, then annoyed, that those words caused a sudden hurt inside her.

There were no chickens on the estate, so for her main course she opted for supreme of chicken with lemon, ginger and lime sauce. She glared at Bryce when he, just to rile her she felt sure, ordered rack of lamb in rosemary and mushroom sauce to follow his starter of lightly poached oysters.

Once Bryce had given the order and suggested they forgo wine with their meal so they could enjoy a liqueur afterwards, he looked hard at Flora and said abruptly, 'I'd like to apologise for my behaviour last night.'

'I never gave it a second's thought,' she assured him, lying valiantly.

Bryce shrugged. 'That's why I tried to catch you at the shop this morning. I wanted to make my apology in person rather than phoning you.' Okay, he was stretching the truth a bit; he'd gone with the intention of asking her to have lunch with him. 'When I heard Rupert mention your date with him . . . ' *I was annoyed.* ' . . . I realised you wouldn't be working your lunch hour and I thought we could meet and talk things through.' He knew he'd been a bit out of order leaving that message with Flora's manageress the minute he'd done it. 'I felt trying to put things right between us was probably more important than you having lunch with Rupert,' he concluded. Though he hadn't been surprised when Flora wasn't at her flat at twelve-thirty.

★   ★   ★

Flora wondered if he realised how . . . how arrogant he sounded, but she couldn't help gloating inwardly; both episodes had merited a mention, and by keeping her cool, Bryce had been forced to be the one to bring them up. And was he also trying to ascertain if she'd kept her date with Rupert after all? She wasn't going to pander to his curiosity, that was for sure.

'I'm glad I didn't make it at lunchtime,' she told him. 'This is a very impressive way of apologising.'

Bryce gave a half-smile. 'When Mother heard the tenants' meeting was off, she took it for granted I'd be seeing you. I couldn't think what to say, so I told her we'd had a bit of an argument. I'm afraid she thought she was the cause of it.'

'Why on earth should she think that?'

Amusement flickered in his eyes. 'She thought you might have taken the huff because she's staying with me for a couple of days.'

Flora shook her head. 'I don't understand. Why — ?'

'She thinks maybe you feel you can't spend time at my place when she's there. After all, as far as she's concerned we're engaged, and engaged couples spend time together. Anyway, that's when she suggested this surprise for you. She planned the whole thing, her phone call to you, and — '

'And you driving Froggie in case I saw your car in the carpark?' Flora seized the chance to get away from hearing about Mrs Torman's thoughts on engaged couples.

His grimace of disgust was a delight

to behold as he shuddered and replied, 'Yes, that too. She's a wily old bird at times.'

'Well, I must admit I feel less guilty about deceiving her now I know what she's capable of,' said Flora. 'And I think I'm going to really enjoy my meal.'

⋆ ⋆ ⋆

Flora's enjoyment of her meal must have been obvious, because Bryce quirked an eyebrow and said, 'Anyone would think you hadn't eaten all day.'

She laughingly admitted that, apart from a slice of toast for breakfast at stupid o'clock and a small cream cake in the middle of the afternoon, she hadn't. Then, catching Bryce's complacent smile and wanting to wipe it off, she said, 'I had better things than food to think of at lunch time,' and gave a complacent smile of her own as she watched Bryce's brows draw together in annoyance.

There. That had made him think she was with Rupert. She'd have to warn Val not to mention she'd been with her instead; that would spoil everything. Though maybe she was being unfair to Bryce. After all, he had apologised. But his apology was more for his behaviour last night than his high-handed attitude in cancelling her lunch date with Rupert. No, she wasn't really being unfair. Bryce needed taking down a peg or two.

Conversation dried up after that. Flora felt relieved when they moved to one of the hotel's cosy corners to drink their coffee and liqueurs. It meant she'd soon be able to leave. She'd almost finished her coffee when Harvey Illing-worth appeared by her chair, an ingratiating smile on his face; the smile being for Bryce, whom Harvey obviously recognised, Flora acknowledged as she reluctantly performed a brief introduction.

'A business meeting, is it?' queried Harvey, showing no inclination to move on. 'If you want a floral set designing for an occasion at Torman Hall, then Flora's the right choice. She did a marvellous job for my mother's masked ball at our country mansion.'

'As it happens, it isn't a business meeting.' Bryce's voice was cold and aloof. 'Flora and I are old friends.'

'Really?' Harvey managed to look disbelieving and impressed at the same time. One could almost see his mind ticking over, almost hear his thoughts: *If it was true* . . . He turned his attention to Flora. 'Haven't seen much of you since Ma's party, my sweet. We must get together again soon.'

Flora cringed and wondered how she could ever have found Harvey's exaggerated cut-glass manner of speaking amusing.

'So, if you've got your diary with you, how about taking a dekko to see when you'd be free?' he continued.

I've suddenly become socially acceptable because I'm with the great Bryce Torman, fumed Flora silently, recalling again the conversation she'd overheard between Harvey and his cousin when she'd been creating a floral set in Mrs Illingworth's ballroom . . .

Their voices had floated down from the minstrels' gallery. Lavinia had asked Harvey who he was bringing to the party. 'Oh, my little passion flower of course,' he'd replied with obvious derision. 'She's quite useful to me at times. She's the in-name amongst the famous and wealthy.'

'I take it there's no sound of wedding bells in that direction then?'

'Give me some credit, Lavinia. A passionate useful relationship is one thing, but marriage to a flower-shop girl wouldn't do much for my upwardly mobile career, now would it?'

At the time, Flora hadn't known what had hurt the most — the implication that she and Harvey had a really close relationship, which they hadn't, or the way he'd classed her as not good enough for him. Needless to say, she'd never been out with him since.

Now Harvey seemed to realise that he'd outstayed his welcome. After muttering something in his grating drawl about phoning her to fix something up, he strolled away.

'I really don't know how you pick them, Flora,' said Bryce. She was about to agree with him when he added, 'There's not much to choose from between him and my cousin Rupert. They're both full of false charm. Surely you can do better than either of them?'

'At least neither of them behaved the way you did last night,' Flora said. 'They may be full of false charm, but they're both more of a gentleman than you.' She rose from her chair and looked down at him. 'Thank you for the meal, Bryce. *That* was most enjoyable. But I do hope you won't ever feel the need to apologise again. No, don't bother getting up, I can fetch my coat myself.'

And, forcing herself not to look back at him, she walked over to the coatstand, grabbed her coat and, shrugging into it, headed for the exit.

6

Bryce phoned the day after their meal at the hotel and asked Flora if she wanted to call off the whole idea of their masquerade. She informed him coldly that she'd love to, having spent most of the night vowing to do that very thing; but only that morning she'd received an invitation for both of them from Yasem, so they'd have to keep up the pretence a bit longer.

'I can understand Yasem wanting to see you again,' Bryce stated, 'but I can't quite fathom why he included me in his invitation.'

'It wouldn't be right for him to entertain an engaged woman without her fiancé being present. Actually,' she added, relenting slightly, 'he wants us to meet his sister. She's an artist. Yasem showed me some photos of her paintings; you'll like them, Bryce. In fact, he's offered one for the charity auction.'

Bryce was one of the organisers of the well-attended charity auction that was held annually at a prestigious venue in the area. Dozens of local firms and craftspeople took part — not entirely for altruistic reasons, as the publicity was tremendous — auctioning their work or services to the highest bidders.

It would be Flora's fourth year of contributing. She auctioned Daisy Chain's party design service, creating a set for the client and providing the flowers, the payment offered being higher than the usual fee because it would go to the chosen charity. She also stipulated that after the successful bidder's party had taken place, the flowers would be sent to the local hospice, as were the flowers displayed on her stand on the night of the auction.

Yasem's invitation was for the coming Sunday; both Flora and Bryce agreed there was no need for them to see each other until then. If the family thought it strange they weren't together much, the pressure of work could be used as an excuse. 'But I'll pick you up on Sunday,' said Bryce. 'It wouldn't do for us to arrive in separate vehicles.'

In fact, in Flora's case, the pressure of work was a reality as she frantically strove to make sure her new shop would be opening on time. Luckily Pippa, the florist she'd employed to work at Daisy Chain's third shop, had been a great help when one crisis after another presented itself.

And Flora did manage to see Rupert. He took her out for lunch and then on to his showrooms where she bought, at cost price, the unusual urns he'd told her about.

Out of ten days, she and Bryce were only together twice — once when they met with Yasem and his sister, and once when Bryce's uncle, complaining that he'd seen nothing of the happy couple together, commanded their presence at a small dinner party. Both occasions were pleasant enough, as though an unspoken truce had been declared. But Flora's mother, present at the dinner party, commented afterwards on what good actors Flora and Bryce were.

'Nobody could have guessed there was anything between you. Still,' she added brightly, 'I suppose that was just as well, seeing as the editor of the local paper was a guest. And everything will change once Christmas and Val's wedding is over. You'll be announcing your engagement publicly then, won't you? Not a minute too soon, if you ask me. It might put a stop to Jilly Joy's phone calls. She phones Bryce every day.'

'How do you know?' Flora asked, mainly to keep her mother off the subject of herself and Bryce.

'All phone calls to the Hall come through my office during the day,' Mrs Grant reminded her daughter. 'And at least half of them are from Jilly Joy.'

'Oh, well, as you said, after Val's wedding . . . ' Flora busied herself with putting on her coat to avoid her mother's eyes and added silently, *Bryce and I will announce that our engagement is off.*

★ ★ ★

On the evening of the charity auction, the urns Flora had bought from Rupert were put to full use on her stand. She was more than satisfied with her magnificent flower display and felt a warm glow when Bryce, resplendent in formal dress, spent a few minutes admiring it. She felt an even warmer glow, but didn't have time to wonder why, when he told her how pretty she was looking.

However, her evening was ruined for her when both Harvey and Rupert joined in the bidding for the offered party design. Bryce watched with arrogance and scarcely veiled amusement that infuriated Flora as Harvey and Rupert fought to outdo each other, bidding the most ridiculous amounts of money.

It's all in a good cause, thought Flora, a smile pinned to her aching face; but she couldn't fail to notice the contemplative looks being cast her way. And when the hammer fell finally on Harvey's bid, she kept smiling as he swaggered over to her.

'Call in at the local Daisy Chain and arrange everything with Sue, my manageress,' she said briskly to Harvey, disliking the way he was looking at her.

'I don't want Sue, I want you,' Harvey stated belligerently, a nasty expression appearing suddenly on his face. 'I bid for *you*, Flora, not your manageress.'

'You'll find her work excellent,' Flora assured him. 'A lot of the arrangements I used for your mother's masked ball were to Sue's design.'

'I repeat, I bid for you,' Harvey said, his voice beginning to rise.

'Wrong, Mr Illingworth.' Bryce had appeared as if from nowhere; he'd spoken calmly enough, but his very stance showed he'd stand for no argument. 'You bid for, and will receive, a party set designed and arranged by Daisy Chain. Exactly what's stated here.' He pointed to Flora's banner on which, in big fancy print, was her lot number and details of what was being offered.

Flora, remembering the look on Bryce's face when he'd watched the bidding, wasn't too sure if she felt grateful for his intervention. She sneaked a quick look from under her lashes; she couldn't read anything on his face this time, though she had a strong suspicion he might be secretly relishing the situation.

'Sorry, my mistake,' countered Harvey, and Flora tensed at the tone in his voice. Even so, she wasn't prepared for his following words as he leaned toward Bryce and stated, 'You want to be careful about offering friendship to the little passion flower here, old man. She has a habit of getting ideas above her station — or should I say flower bed? Just thought — '

He didn't have time to say any more; Bryce took his arm in a firm grip and, with a pleasant smile on his face, guided him across the lushly carpeted room. The group of people bidding for the next item automatically formed a passageway, an usher opened the heavy oak door, and Harvey was escorted out of the building.

Flora, feeling physically sick and guessing her face would be stark white, fought to regain her composure. Thank heavens nobody else had been close enough to hear Harvey's words. But what had Bryce made of them? Her eyes fastened on his tall figure as he re-entered the room.

He stood head and shoulders above the crowd, but he didn't as much as glance over in her direction. Was that because he was despising her? She couldn't bear him to think that she and Harvey . . . But, she reminded herself bitterly, Bryce, in part at least, had made a similar statement years ago.

And when had it started to matter what Bryce thought of her?

'Wow, I'm glad I stopped bidding

when I did.' Rupert arrived bearing a glass of non-alcoholic wine for Flora, and she was grateful that she'd no more time to think about Harvey's vicious, suggestive words or what Bryce was thinking.

'I didn't know the highest bidder also won Bryce's services as an escort.' Rupert grinned wickedly. Then, obviously noticing Flora's discomfort, he dropped a friendly arm around her shoulder. 'Listen, love, I'm sorry for my part in that ostentatious exhibition. I realise now it only served to show you up. And Cousin Bryce didn't seem — '

'Forget it, Rupert,' Flora interrupted desperately. 'I'm trying to.'

'Okay, we'll talk about something else,' he agreed, pushing the wine glass into Flora's hand. 'I came across another urn today and thought you might like it for your new shop. You're opening in a couple of days, aren't you? Good timing, that, so soon after tonight's little bash.'

'It was unintentional,' Flora responded

with a weak smile. 'It just worked out that way. I'd planned my original opening date for a couple of weeks ago, but there were a few delays. However, now it's so soon after this, it did make it easier to persuade the local paper to give me a write-up. They're actually sending a photographer along on my opening day.'

She'd heard her own words; they'd sounded flat and monotonous. She had felt the effort she'd made to form them, but still felt as if someone else had spoken them.

'Speaking of photographers, here comes one now,' observed Rupert. 'I expect I'll be dubbed the unlucky loser. On second thought,' he added abruptly, 'I think I'll make myself scarce. I see Bryce striding this way, too. And I don't like the look in his eyes. I'll call in to see you in the morning.' And after giving her shoulder a brief squeeze, he hurried off.

'I really would have thought, Flora,' Bryce said, 'that the display your two boyfriends subjected you to would have brought you to your senses. But no — Rupert, free and easy with his affections as usual, is calling in on you in the morning.'

'What was I supposed to do? Refuse to talk to Rupert and draw attention to myself again? Besides, he was apologising to me.'

'You didn't have to embrace in public or make a date with him.'

Rupert's arm around her shoulder had hardly been an embrace, and it had been Rupert making the date, but she didn't bother to point that out. Bryce had no right to act and speak like this; no right to be looking at her like this with a kind of sad anger, she thought confusedly. No right, either, to make her feel as if she wanted to seek comfort by burying her head against his broad chest and feel forgiving arms around her. She hadn't done anything to forgive, for heaven's sake.

'Don't think I haven't heard about your disgusting display,' she flashed, anger coming to her rescue. 'Drinking champagne out of the slipper Cinderella, otherwise known as Jilly Joy, threw into your eager hand at the show the other night.'

Flora hadn't intended to mention that episode, which Sue had witnessed when she'd taken her nephew to see Cinderella. Sue, all goggle-eyed, had told Flora about it the following day. And now Flora furiously used it against this arrogant being who had the cheek to criticise her.

'Could I just have a smile from you, please?' begged the harassed photographer. Flora had been vaguely aware of him bobbing up and down for a good few minutes trying to get an acceptable photo.

I'll smile when this contemptuous creature leaves me alone, Flora replied silently.

Bryce laughed harshly, clearly guessing exactly what she was thinking. He gave her a mock bow and told the poor photographer that the lady was now all his.

'Don't know why he looked so mad,' said the photographer. 'As one of the organisers, Mr Torman should be delighted at how much money you made for the charity. That was some bidding, that was. Never seen anything like it.'

'Me neither,' Flora agreed despondently. 'Now, how about you taking your photo, then I can dismantle this lot and get home.' She felt like a rag doll with its stuffing falling out, and didn't think she could take much more of this evening.

* * *

The photographer had departed, having at last managed to take his photos, and Flora was carefully removing her flowers from the urns, counting each one to prevent herself from thinking, and placing them in buckets ready for delivery to the hospice. She could hear the background buzz of conversation, but the auctioning had obviously finished. She wondered bleakly if she dared leave before Bryce made his usual speech, when he thanked everyone for giving up part of their Saturday evening and for their generosity, followed by an announcement of the grand total.

Leaning back on her heels, she decided glumly that she'd have to stay until the bitter end. Then she felt a light touch on her shoulder. 'Flora, I'll do that for you.'

'I was wondering when you'd remember your promise to help me, Val.' Flora glanced up at her friend. 'Did you get a good price for your books? I couldn't hear the bidding very well from here with you being right at the other end of the room.' Once again, she felt as if someone else had spoken her words for her.

'Yes, yes, I did. Never mind that for now. For heaven's sake, go and talk to Bryce. Jilly Joy has just arrived and she's drooling all over him.'

'So? Let her. I'm fed up with your

brother and his double standards.'

'You don't understand,' Val almost wailed, crouching down beside Flora. 'Quentin is here and Yasem is with him. He wanted to watch his sister's painting being auctioned. He did, and now he's watching Bryce and Jilly Joy. He looks quite disgusted. Flora, please go over to Bryce.'

Feeling fed up with her best friend, too, Flora stood up. 'Where are they?' she asked, resigned to complying with Val's request.

Val pointed them out and, sighing deeply, Flora made her way across the room. 'Excuse me, Mr Torman, but I have a message from your sister. Her fiancé and his friend would like a word with you. They're over there where the paintings were displayed.'

'Thank you, Miss Grant. I'd like a word with you, as it happens. Perhaps you'd stroll in that direction with me?' He didn't wait for a reply. He disentangled Jilly Joy from his body, whispered something in her ear, and then put his hand under Flora's elbow to guide her away.

Earlier, she'd wanted to feel his touch. Now she dearly wanted to push his hand away from her, but was worried Yasem night see.

'I didn't know Yasem was coming.' Bryce bent his head towards her, moving closer in the process.

'Nor did I.' Her voice was tense and oddly constrained. *Nothing to do with the fact he's so close to me,* she told herself, and resorted to bitter sarcasm as she added, 'Such a nice surprise having to play the engaged couple again. But I think you'd better explain to Yasem that you're only interested in Jilly's cows.'

'I'm glad you said Jilly's cows and not just cows,' he drawled, and then laughed at Flora's snort of anger.

But suddenly and unexpectedly, Flora found herself saying, 'There was never anything more than a couple of kisses between me and Harvey Illingworth.'

'What makes you think I'm interested in your love life or lack of it?' He whispered the last words in to her ear.

Just as he'd whispered in Jilly Joy's ear, fumed Flora. But she didn't know whether it was that, or what he'd said, causing her anger. She'd no time to reply, even if she'd been capable of so doing. Yasem had moved forward to greet them.

Whatever had happened earlier was nothing to this last half-hour spent being polite to Yasem and sweet to Bryce. Not only that, but suffering his odd 'loving' touches on her hand; having to return his 'loving' looks; having to lean against him when he casually pulled her closer to him, his hands resting lightly on her waist. But Flora, to her secret horror, again found herself wishing Bryce's loving act was for real. Then promptly and gratefully scorned that wish when Bryce politely declined Yasem's suggestion that he and Flora join him, Val and Quentin for a meal.

'I'm looking forward to a quiet supper just for two,' Bryce explained charmingly.

Flora knew Bryce didn't mean him and her. Hurt and anger churned away inside as she pictured Bryce's quiet supper with Jilly Joy. Though it was the anger that threatened to overspill when, after Yasem smilingly commented on the fact that the thought of a quiet supper had certainly brought a sparkle to Flora's eyes, Bryce chuckled and, looking deeply into them, said, 'Yes, your eyes are sparkling,' and immediately excused himself gracefully, as it was time for him to make his speech.

7

Flora lay back on the sofa, eyes closed, Beethoven's 'Moonlight Sonata' playing softly in the background. She knew she'd have to unwind before she went to bed and attempted to sleep. Knew, too, that she'd have to start controlling her temper.

Living in a state of almost perpetual anger as she had been doing over the last couple of weeks — or at least whenever Bryce was around, she amended — was draining her energy. She should be well and truly immune to him by now, and shouldn't have to use anger to enforce that immunity. The trouble was, using anger against him had become a habit. That habit would have to be broken, as they couldn't spend the rest of the month — Val's wedding rehearsals, Christmas and Boxing Day, the estate workers' party, the wedding itself . . .

'We can't spend all that time in a state of anger with each other. Yes . . . *We, each other*,' she murmured. 'Because Bryce gets just as angry as I do. Why?'

She opened her eyes and stared up at the ceiling as though she might find some answers there. *Does he just react to my anger with his own, or is his there already? Does he have another reason for it? Is he using it to hide some other feeling? Is he trying to control, to deny a physical feeling for me as I am for him?*

'No,' she groaned aloud, sitting bolt upright. 'I am not still attracted to him after all these years. I'm not. I'm not.'

Liar, mocked her innermost self. *Look how you responded to him on the night of Val's party.*

'That was an act,' she said. 'I thought one of the family were there.'

Come off it, Flora. That annoying inner voice would not shut up. *You could have stopped him; you said yourself that nobody could see into the hall. You were enjoying it; you felt bereft when Bryce released you. And he was the one to stop, not you. You didn't even struggle at the end of the evening, after the party, when he kissed you in a temper.*

'I couldn't have stopped him then. He was using his superior strength against me,' Flora argued back. 'Anyway, now be quiet,' she told her intrusive inner self. 'I need to think.'

She got up and turned the record over — she still preferred vinyl to any other — and then sank onto the carpet and leaned back against an armchair. All right, she was attracted to Bryce; but she was no longer an impressionable teenager of sixteen, for heaven's sake. She should be able to handle those feelings now. Handle them without resorting to anger or a bad temper.

The night he'd tricked her into meeting him at the hotel . . . well, she'd managed to act coolly and calmly — at least until she'd walked out. And she'd managed okay when they'd both gone to Yasem's, and again at Uncle Hector's dinner party. That proved she could do it, and it was what she'd do from now on, she vowed. Act coolly and calmly.

As for Bryce . . . It was ridiculous to think he was attracted to her in any way. The first time he'd kissed her, on that occasion it had been more of an almost-kiss really, all those years ago in the hay loft. He'd been teasing and tormenting her, and had been quick enough to point out it shouldn't have happened.

Tormenting her as well, the times after that — last year under the mistletoe, and more recently on the night of Val's party. Yes, every time he'd been tormenting her, setting out to rouse her anger; and she'd played into his hands. Hands which she'd pleasured in the touch of as they'd lingered on her waist a couple of hours earlier, she recalled uneasily. But she wouldn't be seeing him until Val's wedding rehearsal on Thursday. By then she might have forgotten the way he'd made her feel tonight; might actually wonder how she could have wished, even briefly, that his loving act had been for real. Though as a safeguard, she'd just have to make sure that Bryce didn't get close to her. Appropriately, the record came to an end and, glancing at the time, she saw it was eleven o'clock.

'I think I'll make a mug of hot chocolate and drink a toast to the new cool and calm Flora Grant,' she murmured. 'And then I'll go to bed.'

Once in the kitchen, and feeling slightly more at ease with herself, Flora realised she was hungry. She popped some crumpets under the grill, and had just filled the kettle and was about to switch it on, when the intercom on her kitchen wall buzzed. Somebody was ringing the bell to her flat. It could only be Harvey, she reckoned grimly. Come to make more trouble. She threw up a silent prayer of thanks for the security system that enabled her to know who was outside before she allowed them access. She certainly would not let Harvey Illingworth into the building.

She replied to the second buzz with a terse, 'Yes?'

'Flora . . . ?' It was Bryce's voice, not Harvey's. 'I've got Val's keys and I'm coming up.'

A furious retort rose to her lips but she bit it down. Cool and calm, she reminded herself, and managed a disinterested, 'Okay.' At least he'd made her aware of his intention. Seeing as he had Val's keys, he could have just walked in.

'I'm in the kitchen,' she called when she heard the front door open, and felt proud of her detached tone. Nevertheless, she wasn't breathing too easily; and although she didn't turn round, she knew from the prickling sensation at the back of her neck the very second he appeared in the doorway.

'I thought it might scare you out of your wits if I just let myself in without warning you.'

Recognising the teasing note in his

voice, and knowing he must be expecting a fiery response, she forced herself to stay silent and not to turn and look at him.

She detected an underlying puzzled tone in his next words. 'I knew you were still up. I walked round the back and saw the lights on.'

'Mmm.' She still didn't turn. 'I'm making crumpets and hot chocolate. Do you want some?'

'I've brought our meal with me. Seeing as you disappeared before I could tell you I'd booked a table at the Italian restaurant, I made use of their take-out service. Why *did* you disappear, Flora? You heard me tell Yasem I was looking forward to having supper with you.'

But he hadn't, had he? He hadn't actually mentioned her name. He must have known, given that she'd interrupted his dalliance with Jilly Joy, that she'd think it was Jilly he was taking for a meal. Now Flora wanted to turn and yell at him, wanted to throw something at him, to . . . No. She'd play him at his own game.

So she turned to look at him. His body seemed to fill the doorway as he leaned casually against the jamb, holding the packaged food. His dark hair was slightly ruffled, his grey cashmere overcoat unbuttoned. He was still wearing his formal suit, but he'd taken off his tie and his shirt was open at the neck.

She was appalled at how her heart pounded as she looked at him, and swallowed hard trying to alleviate the dryness of her mouth. *I must say something*, she thought frantically as he stood there watching her with a quizzical expression on his face.

'I . . . I didn't know you meant it,' she managed finally. 'About supper together, I mean. I thought — '

'The crumpets,' he interrupted urgently. 'On fire.'

She swung round, grabbed the grill pan, threw it into the sink and turned the cold water on. Somehow Bryce was right behind her, snatching her hands and holding them away from the heat. 'You little fool,' he said. 'You could have got a really bad burn doing that.'

'Well I didn't,' she retorted, flustered by his nearness and by the way her skin was prickling, which had nothing to do with the sizzling heat from the charred crumpets. 'I'm all right, Bryce. You can let go of my hands.'

But he'd pulled her round and was now holding both her hands in one of his, the other gently lifting her chin so she had to look at him. To her dismay, she felt her eyes fill with tears, and tried in vain to prevent them from falling.

'Dammit all, don't cry, Flora. I'm sorry, I didn't mean to yell at you. I just couldn't bear to think of you being hurt. For heaven's sake, why do we always seem to resort to anger with each other?' He didn't let go of her, but he moved the hand from under her chin to stroke her tears away.

'Listen,' he said quietly, 'when I first mentioned it to Yasem, it was just talk; I hadn't planned on us two having a meal together. Then I thought it might be a good idea after all. I thought we could try and talk about things and maybe agree not to keep losing our tempers with each other.'

'I'd been thinking the same thing just before you arrived,' Flora admitted. 'I'm sick and tired of being angry all the time. But you keep tormenting me,' she added under her breath.

Bryce must have heard, though, for he nodded and said, 'It's habit, I think. I've been doing it for years.'

'We both have.' Tremulously, she shared the responsibility. 'I think in my case, it's because as long as I've known you, you've treated me like an annoying younger sister. You stopped treating Val like that as we grew up but continued to torment me almost every time we set eyes on each other. And I — '

'And you responded by getting mad. But I didn't torment you every time,' he denied, his fingers now toying with her hair. 'Do you remember that day when you told your mother you were thinking of having a spa-bath installed?'

'Mmm. I was in her office at Torman Hall. I'd just bought the flat and I'd driven over there specially to show her the brochures for the bath. All she showed was disapproval. Until . . . until you walked into the office, glanced over her shoulder and started enthusing about the merits of spa-baths. But Bryce, if you'd known you were agreeing with me, you wouldn't have said what you did.'

'Not true. I'd been listening outside the door. Not purposely — I was about to come in and ask your mother for some figures I needed; but when I heard your voice and noticed that you were trying so hard to be reasonable, I couldn't resist listening to what you were saying. I don't know why I did what I did. I suppose I suddenly felt that for once I wanted to support you.'

'And my mother changed her mind and agreed it was a good idea after all. But why didn't you tell me afterwards that you'd overheard me and her talking?'

'Oh, I don't know.' He shrugged. 'I suppose the next time we met I was back to teasing you. You always rise so easily, and . . . To tell you the truth, Flora, you look beautiful when you're annoyed.' Then quickly, as though regretting that last remark, he dropped his hands, stepped away from her and said, 'Now . . . ' He indicated the packages he'd thrown on the table when the crumpets had caught fire. 'How about popping Mario's pasta in the microwave?'

As they ate, they started to recall other times when they hadn't been at each other's throats: the night Flora had seen a stray dog savaging a newborn lamb, and how Bryce had shed a tear along with her when he'd had to put the lamb out of its misery. The ewe has produced another lamb but had rejected it. Bryce and Flora fought to keep the tiny creature alive, and had won the battle.

'Remember that time much further back when Uncle Hector was going to cane me for riding a cow?' Bryce's face lit up with amusement. 'You came running into his study, bent over next to me and said he'd better cane you as well, because you'd ridden her too.'

Flora giggled. 'It worked, didn't it? Stopped him from caning you, I mean; because he couldn't very well cane me.'

'How old were you then?'

'About seven, I think.'

'Which means I was sixteen and old enough to know better. But had you really ridden a cow?'

'No. Believe it or not, I was a frightened of cows at that age.' She took the last mouthful of delicious pasta and pushed her empty plate to one side before continuing. 'I didn't really do it to save your neck, but to try and curry favour with you. Val and I had been fooling around with one of your model planes; a wing fell off and we stuck it back on. We weren't too sure if we'd got it in the right place. I thought if I could

140

stop your uncle Hector from caning you . . . '

'You and Val would have a bargaining point if I found out about the plane.' Bryce laughed. 'So devious at only seven years old. I'll take a look at my models sometime. I've still got them all.'

'I've still got His Patchiness,' Flora confessed.

'That moth-bitten teddy bear?'

'You're responsible for most of his patches. You ran the tractor over him and he got caught in the wheels.'

'That was because you turned the hosepipe on me. But let's only talk about the times we didn't argue and fall out.'

They managed to recall quite a few, and it seemed fairly easy to make a pact to get through the rest of the month without any rows.

'And maybe *that* will become habit,' said Bryce. 'Maybe we'll be able to remain good friends even after Val's wedding, too.'

'You mean when we can stop pretending we're secretly engaged?'

'I think we'll have to keep up the pretence for a little while after the wedding.'

Flora felt her heart beat a small tattoo of happiness which promptly stopped when Bryce continued, 'Let the family down gently. I've got a feeling our mothers will be slightly upset. For some reason they seem to think we're perfect for each other. Ridiculous, isn't it.'

He quirked an eyebrow and a pain like a knife twisting inside her shot through Flora as she agreed that it was indeed ridiculous.

* * *

What was even more ridiculous, Flora mused later — much later, when Bryce was long gone and she was trying in vain to get to sleep — was the fact that she'd agreed to spend the next afternoon with Bryce; just the two of them, so they could get used to being together without arguing. At least, that had been Bryce's reason for the suggestion. 'A sort of continuation of our quiet supper together' was how he'd put it.

Her reason for agreeing to it didn't quite tally with his, she admitted ruefully. She must be some sort of masochist, but she wanted to be alone with Bryce just for the sheer pleasure of being with him — hearing his voice, watching his movements, catching a tantalising drift of his cologne as he walked past her — even if, in reality, that pleasure was pain.

Gone was her resolution of not letting him close. She wanted to feel his arm around her; wanted the touch of his lips. Her teenage crush had never really died; it had matured and grown into a much deeper feeling.

* * *

Flora woke early and found herself wondering how she'd get through the hours until it was time to go to Torman

Hall — counting the hours until she'd see Bryce, acting like a lovelorn teen. Which only went to show, she thought, half-annoyed and half-amused, that she hadn't really matured that much at all. And she was leaving herself open to heartache, so why was she letting her heart rule her head?

'It's nothing but physical attraction, not even reciprocated. Bryce just wants us to try and be good friends.' She spoke the words aloud, trying to make them more meaningful. Because this time, 'good friends' meant exactly that.

Bryce hadn't even air-kissed her goodbye last night. When he'd looked down at her, he'd said 'Let's seal the bargain,' using the same words as once before. That time she'd fought off his kiss. Last night she would have welcomed it, but Bryce had held out a hand and shaken hers to seal the bargain.

She groaned at her perversity and, jumping out of bed, decided with mock humour that she'd spend the morning cleaning the flat. That would pass the time and maybe take her mind off other things.

She'd forgotten Rupert's promise to call, but was selfishly delighted when he arrived at noon and suggested going for a pub lunch, adding that it couldn't be too long a lunch as he had an appointment in Chester later on.

Even so, Flora still felt slightly guilty at the look of pleasure and approval in his eyes when she returned from changing her flat-cleaning clothes, after settling him with a coffee. Guilty because she'd dressed not for her lunch with Rupert but for her afternoon with Bryce. She was wearing a softly flowing light woollen skirt in a riot of colours, teamed with a cream silk blouse and a soft angora jumper which exactly matched her sage-green suede boots. She'd sprayed on her favourite 'Bamboo' perfume, and her hair, held in place with two side-combs, fell behind her shoulders in honey-gold waves.

'All this for me?' Rupert queried

lightly, rising from the chair.

'Not entirely,' she replied honestly. 'I'm going on somewhere after our lunch.'

'Don't look so contrite,' he joked. 'I'll benefit from your appearance too. I'll be the envy of every hot-blooded male in the pub. They aren't to know that we'll be going our own separate ways when we leave.'

Impatient though she was to be with Bryce, she did enjoy her lunch. Rupert was an amusing companion. They got on well together; and although he flirted lightly, they both knew there was no real attraction between them.

Strange how it happens like this sometimes, pondered Flora. *Rupert's a good-looking virile male, he's got a great sense of humour, we've a lot in common, and we look good together yet neither of us wants anything more from our relationship. Why can't I feel this way about Bryce? It would make things so much easier.*

★ ★ ★

Two hours later, the only feelings she had towards Bryce were dislike and contempt. She'd driven round to the back of Torman Hall and was surprised to see a huge, obviously very expensive motorbike parked there. Curiously wondering to whom it could belong, she didn't look upwards until she'd parked her car and got out. Looking down at her from halfway up the stone steps leading to Bryce's front door was Bryce himself — arm in arm with a black leather-clad Jilly Joy.

So, realised Flora, Bryce had obviously arranged to see Jilly. 'That's why he suggested me coming here this afternoon,' she muttered. It was so she could act as 'chaperone'. If Hector Torman happened to be aware of Jilly's presence, he wouldn't think anything of it if his nephew's fiancée was also there.

What a despicable, lying creature Bryce is, fumed Flora, leaping back into her car and driving away with a screech of tyres. *How dare he insult me like this? All that nonsense about us getting* used to being with each other without arguing, and I fell for it. I actually believed he meant it; believed he wanted us to try and be friends. Huh. I'd rather be friends with a pit full of hissing snakes.

But I've come to my senses once and for all. Val or no Val, the farcical secret engagement between me and Bryce is broken as from now. If Val feels she still needs to prove to Yasem and her uncle Hector that there's nothing between her brother and Jilly Joy, she can just find some other way of doing it. In fact, I'll go and tell her that now.

★ ★ ★

Val's begging and pleading didn't change Flora's mind. She was adamant. She would not continue to live a lie not even for Val.

'I've done my bit, Val. Yasem thinks Bryce and I are secretly engaged and there's no way he'll find out we're not. I won't be seeing Yasem, and when you

148

do you're hardly likely to mention it.'

'He's coming to the wedding reception.'

'You said the contracts will be signed before the wedding, so that's okay. Bryce and I won't need to pretend anything.'

'There's some sort of hitch,' Val said. 'Oh, nothing serious, but it might delay the signing until New Year. And that could mean — '

'Look — if the contracts haven't been signed, then I'll stay away from the reception. I'll invent an illness — appendicitis, anything. But I — '

'But you're my best friend. I can't get married without you being there.'

'Oh, Val.' Flora leaped up and hugged her. 'I'll still be your chief bridesmaid; and I won't let my feelings for Bryce wreck the wedding ceremony, I promise. But I can't come to the reception if it means acting a part for Yasem. After the trick Bryce tried to pull, I wouldn't even be able to pretend to *like* him, let alone anything else.'

'All right. But you do promise you'll

still be my chief bridesmaid no matter what else happens?'

'I've just told you I will.'

'So you'll keep your final dress fitting appointment?'

'Yes.'

'And come to the wedding rehearsal on Thursday? Bryce will be there of course, but everybody will be concentrating on me and Quentin.'

'I'll be there. I can disappear quickly once the rehearsal's over.'

'I just wish I could be sure that on the day itself you'll come to the reception,' said Val.

'If the contracts are signed and I don't have to pretend I'm engaged to your despicable brother, I'll come to the reception as well. That's the best I can say, Val.'

★   ★   ★

Flora had never been so grateful for her work as she was during the next two days. There wasn't much time to think about Bryce and how she'd almost let herself fall under his charismatic spell again.

She'd heard no word from him; and when she'd phoned her mother, something had interrupted their conversation almost before it had started, so his name hadn't been mentioned by either of them. She'd have to tell her mother the truth soon, though. Perhaps Thursday, after the wedding rehearsal, would be the best time. Bryce could break the news to his mother and uncle then as well.

She did sometimes wonder if Val had told Bryce that the farce was at an end. And then wondered why Bryce hadn't contacted her. In the odd spare moment, she also recalled Harvey's behaviour and implications on the night of the auction. Ironically, it was thanks to Bryce that the Harvey episode hadn't lingered to haunt her. But the disgust she felt for Bryce's behaviour far outweighed her annoyance with Harvey.

On the whole, the imminent opening of her latest flower boutique took precedence. On Tuesday, as promised, the local newspaper sent a photographer along with their reporter, and Flora was promised good coverage.

'This will be a follow-on to the piece on the charity auction. We've earmarked a slot for tomorrow's issue. We do our best to give the December issues a happy slant,' the reporter confided. 'Christmastime should be happy.'

'Yes, it should,' agreed Flora, wondering how her own Christmas could possibly be happy under the circumstances, before firmly telling herself she'd make sure it was. She wouldn't allow her disillusionment with Bryce to affect her, she told herself once the reporter had left. Though she couldn't fathom why she should feel so disillusioned. Bryce hadn't actually acted out of character when he'd resorted to trickery and deceit to get her to see him.

A flurry of customers diverted her thoughts, and once again she was grateful for having her work to concentrate on.

8

What with my dress fitting this after-noon and the wedding rehearsal tonight, I could do without having to make an extra trip to the flower market, thought Flora as she buttered a couple of pieces of toast. *Still, I shouldn't grumble. Almost selling out on the first day open was pretty good, and Pippa worked really hard. She's going to be an ideal manager.*

Flora hadn't had the heart to refuse when Pippa had suggested going for a meal and a little drink to celebrate. When she'd got home, she'd felt so tired she hadn't bothered to check the answering machine for messages. Nibbling on a slice of toast, she hurried into the hall and activated the machine. She smiled when she heard her mother's plaintive 'I hate talking on these things,' then frowned at the next words: 'In case Bryce hasn't had time to contact you, I thought I'd just set your mind at rest, poppet. We know all about it now, the panic's over, and everything will be all right. I'll see you at the wedding rehearsal; we'll talk then.'

'That's great,' Flora said aloud. She supposed Yasem and Quentin must have overcome the hitch and signed the contracts. Val might have let her know. Though to be fair, she could have phoned and got no response — Flora hadn't had her personal mobile switched on much. Still, Val had obviously told Bryce, and he wasted no time in explaining things to the family.

'And Bryce must be very busy if he couldn't find the time to tell me we can stop putting on an act,' she said as she walked back into the kitchen.

It was one for the history books, though — a pretend secret engagement that lasted nineteen days. Shrugging, Flora sat at the table, finished her breakfast and then went to get dressed.

I wonder what Mother meant by 'everything will be all right'? she pondered as she pulled on the quilted dungarees she wore for her market trips. *Has Uncle Hector accepted Bryce's carrying on with Jilly Joy, or has Bryce stopped carrying on with her?*

'Why should I care anyway?' she admonished herself, trying to banish from her mind the picture of the black-leather-clad Jilly Joy and Bryce standing arm in arm on the steps leading to his front door. It was all so easy to imagine them walking into his home, into his . . .

'I don't care if he made love to her. I really, really don't,' she said forcefully, glaring at her reflection in the mirror. 'Bryce 'Torment' is a despicable, deceitful, double-talking devil. So there,' she finished childishly, sticking her tongue out at herself before laughing ruefully.

Deciding she wouldn't give him another second's thought, she hurried out of the flat and down the stairs. On opening the main door, a dark, bleak morning greeted her; a perfect match for her mood.

*   *   *

'But why the heck don't I feel better now the need for pretence is over?' Flora muttered in exasperation half an hour later as she drove her well-known route to the market.

She knew the answer really. It was because Bryce had inveigled his way into her heart again, and this time it was going to be harder to shut him out. The Christmas party wouldn't be too hard to cope with, as there'd be plenty of people to use as a barrier between them. But at Val's wedding — and, heavens, the wedding rehearsal tonight — there'd be nothing to act as a barrier then except herself.

'I've done it before, and I'll do it again,' she said aloud. 'I'll be my own barrier.'

And, in this positive frame of mind, she parked her car and concentrated her thoughts on selecting the flowers and other items she needed. She bought extra stock for all three of her flower boutiques and, as it wasn't a day she normally did the market run, she had to unload on her own at the first two as the staff hadn't been expecting her so hadn't yet arrived.

Pippa was expecting her, though, and was there when Flora drew up. 'Congratulations, Flora,' she called, running up and not even giving Flora time to open the Range Rover's door. 'Marvellous pictures, and the newspaper's given you a fantastic write-up.'

'Haven't even seen it yet,' replied Flora, getting out of the car with a smile for Pippa's enthusiasm. 'But it's the reporter and the photographer you should be congratulating if it's that good.'

'You've got a centre-page spread. It's so exciting. Why didn't you say anything last night?'

'I didn't know I'd get so much coverage. Come on, Pippa — the sooner we unload this lot, the sooner I can have a look at the paper. Centre-page spread! Must be because I gave them a poinsettia each.'

'He's so good-looking. So much charisma, too.' Pippa sighed as she trundled a pile of boxes into the shop.

'Which one? Photographer or reporter?'

'I wouldn't say either of *them* were exactly tall, dark and to die for like — ' Pippa stopped short as a car pulled up with a screech of brakes. 'Ooh, he's here now. He's even better in the flesh.'

'You've lost me, Pippa,' said Flora, walking towards the counter with her boxes.

'Look,' Pippa demanded, making urgent movements towards the window with her head.

Flora turned and slowly lowered her pile of boxes onto the counter and stared in stunned mystification as Bryce hurtled out of his Ferrari and strode into the shop. He'd been to her other shops before of course, but this was his first visit here. Reined-in anger seemed to emanate from every pore of his body, though the eyes that regarded her held a hurt bewilderment. Something terrible must have happened, thought Flora, taking an uncertain step towards him.

'I want to talk to you, Flora. Let your manager sort everything out,' he demanded in a tone that brooked no argument. Then, taking her arm, he continued, 'Not here. We'll drive somewhere.'

He hadn't raised his voice once; the quiet but meaningful way he'd spoken was far more effective. Flora obeyed him without thought, telling Pippa the keys were in the ignition and asking her to park the Range Rover when she'd finished unloading.

And almost before she knew it, Flora found herself in the passenger seat of Bryce's Ferrari and felt him strapping her seat-belt on. Then, snapping tersely at her not to speak while he was driving, he set off, going through the little town with no regard for the speed limit.

He looks tired, hurt, worn out, bewildered, angry . . . Thoughts went round and round in Flora's head. Surely her mother would have let her know if something serious had happened. *Mum. Something's happened to her*, panicked Flora. But at that moment, Bryce pulled

159

into a lay-by and drew to a halt.

Turning to face her, he grated, 'How could you use this situation for your own personal triumph? It isn't the first time you've used the local paper in your vendetta against me. I still remember the greeting you had printed on one of my birthdays: 'Happy Birthday, Bryce Torment'. You were only a young kid then; now you're supposed to be an adult. But I didn't expect even you to stoop this low, Flora. Two pages of — '

That 'even you' hurt her deeply, but anger easily overcame that as she exploded, 'I can only imagine that you think I used my position as 'a friend of the family' to get the lease on the shop. The shop that's owned by the Torman Estate. No, shut up and let me finish,' she went on as he opened his mouth to interrupt. 'I applied for the lease like anyone else would have done — my solicitors handled the whole thing. They negotiated with your uncle's agent. I doubt your uncle Hector even knew that I'd applied for the lease. And if he *had* known, he'd have judged my application on my business acumen shown by the figures from my first two shops and on the four references I had to provide. I can't understand your problem. You knew which town I was opening my third flower boutique in, and Torman Estate owns many of the shops there. You could have checked to see if mine was one of them if — '

'I'm not talking about you leasing one of our blasted shops,' he roared. 'I'm talking about the two-page announcement.'

'What's wrong with it? If the editor saw fit to devote two pages to my new shop — '

'Flora, if you don't stop this ridiculous act I won't be responsible for my actions. I've had it up to here.' He touched his forehead. 'First the worry over my mother, then this. You do realise that there's no backing out now?'

'Backing out of — ?' she began.

But he cut across her words: 'Your spiteful trick has backfired. It would have been hard enough breaking things off when only the family knew about it. Now that everybody knows, we can't. Mother couldn't take the publicity, the fuss and people asking questions. The stress would probably kill her.'

'Bryce — ' Flora was almost sobbing with frustration. ' — I honestly don't know what you're talking about. What's wrong with your mother, and what spiteful trick are you talking about?'

'You know what's wrong with her. Your mother spoke to you. She told me she had.'

'She left a brief message on my answer machine. From what she said, I thought you'd told them all that we hadn't been engaged after all. But never mind that for now. What's wrong with your mother?'

'She had a bad attack of flu. Her doctor was worried, thought she might be heading for pneumonia, so he sent for me. He sent for me thinking I knew all about Mother's heart condition. But none of us knew anything about it.

She'd kept it to herself for three years.' Suddenly lowering his voice and allowing the weariness and despair to creep in, he continued, 'Anyway, she pulled round and the danger of pneumonia passed just last night. But the doctor told me that any unpleasant shock to her system could be fatal. Oh, Flora, don't you see what you've done by announcing our engagement publicly? There's no way we — '

'Wh-what do you mean, announcing our engagement publicly?' She grabbed his arm and shook it as she continued urgently, 'Who to? When? Where?'

'You really don't know, do you? But I thought . . . ' He ran his fingers through his hair and stared into her face. You haven't seen the write-up in the newspaper, have you?'

'I left home at five o'clock to go to the market for some extra bits and pieces. Bryce, do you mean it says we're engaged? I don't understand. They came to take photos yesterday, and I talked to the reporter about my first two outlets and the name Daisy Chain, but *your* name wasn't mentioned.'

'It does more than say we're engaged,' Bryce said grimly. 'The whole centre spread is devoted to sentences like: *Childhood sweethearts to marry. Love blossoms in the Flower Boutiques. No need for mistletoe.* There are pictures, too,' he added. 'Look, see for yourself.' He reached into the glove compartment, pulled out the newspaper and put it into her hands. 'Pages four and five are devoted to me and Jilly Joy, Jilly admitting she's going to marry the new man in her life. *Is it Bryce Torman?*' he quoted bitterly. 'Then there's the teaser at the bottom.' He jabbed a finger on to the words: *Not Bryce Torman. See centre spread.*'

Flora turned the pages. An enlarged photo of herself and Bryce leapt out at her. 'That was taken at the auction when we were talking to Yasem,' she said. 'And this one . . . ' Her own finger jabbed. 'This one was at the garden party last summer in the grounds of Torman Hall. This one of you standing in my shop doorway . . . they must have used two separate photos and superimposed you onto it.'

The clever captions and the columns of print danced before her eyes and she dragged her gaze away, looking beseechingly into the anger-lined face so close to hers. 'But who? How? Why? I don't understand.' She was vaguely aware she'd said these things earlier, and shook her head. 'Bryce, I swear I was not responsible for this.'

'I believe you, and I'm sorry I accused you. But what else was I to think?' He laid his head against the headrest and closed his eyes. 'I thought by announcing our engagement to one and all you were getting back at not only me but at that lout Harvey Illingworth, too.'

'Getting back at you for what?' Flora asked.

'Jilly Joy last Sunday. I saw your face when you drove away. You were angry, disgusted, and everything else. Quite rightly so, too, if you'd been correct in what I guess your assumption was. But believe it or not — ' He opened his eyes and looked at her. ' — I had no idea that Jilly was coming. It took me two hours to get rid of her. When she finally left, I was just about to pick up the phone to call you, but Mother's doctor phoned me before I had time.'

'Is she going to be all right?'

'She'll have to slow down. And as I said earlier, any shock to her system could be fatal. That's why we'll have to . . . ' He shook his head. 'I just can't think who made that announcement to the newspaper.'

'It must have been Val.'

'Doubtful. She was with me at Mother's, and I'm sure she was too worried about her to think of anything else. We sat up with her for two nights. We didn't manage to get a private nurse until Tuesday. Though I did think Val had let you know where we were and why we were there. I'm sure she said she'd phoned you.'

'She probably tried and couldn't get hold of me,' Flora reasoned. 'It's been a hectic few days. Even my mother didn't get to speak to me. I phoned her once but had to hang up almost straight away, then she left me a message as I told you. And that message makes more sense now. I thought she'd put things rather strangely, thought she was trying to let me know she wasn't annoyed at our pretence. And of course, I understand now why Pippa was talking and acting the way she did this morning.' She sighed and wriggled in her seat, feeling as though she wanted to pace up and down in agitation.

'Flora, I know it's a lot to ask . . . Heck, this is a stupid place to hold a conversation.' Bryce, too, was clearly uncomfortable within the confines of the car, but he continued, 'You must be wishing you'd never heard the name Torman. This is like an extremely bad comedy on TV. First my sister asks you to pretend we're engaged for my sake, then it turns out it was for hers. Now . . . Flora, I'm begging you to go along with it for my mother's sake. Could you bear to for a few months? I know it's asking a lot, I know I've no right to ask you, but — '

'We do go back a long way. Not exactly childhood sweethearts,' Flora added wryly, 'but I couldn't knowingly do something that would put your mother's life at risk.'

'Like asking the paper to print a retraction?'

'Exactly,' she confirmed bleakly. 'At least, an immediate retraction is out of the question. The fuss and media coverage that would incur doesn't bear thinking about. But we can't — '

'I know. We can't stay engaged for-ever. I promise, Flora, I'll get us out of this mess as soon as I can, without causing too much upset for my mother. It's going to be tough while it does last; we'll have to put on an act in front of everyone, not just the family. There's the Christmas party, Val's wedding, and heaven knows what else at this time of year. I'll have to buy you an engagement ring.'

'Bryce, I don't want to talk anymore right now.' Flora's voice trembled, she felt hot and cold at the same time, her throat felt dry, and tears pricked at the corners of her eyes. It was all too much. 'Just drive me back, will you? I've got a lot to do, and my final dress fitting is this afternoon.'

A loud silence filled the car; then, contrarily, she felt as though she couldn't bear the quietness. 'What about Val's wedding? Will your mother be well enough? Val would be heartbroken if — '

'She'll be there, in a wheelchair if necessary. Though it won't be. Put your seatbelt back on, Flora,' he instructed, snapping his own on and starting the car. Then he continued, 'Mother's well on the road to recovery from the flu. And she's lived with her heart condition these last three years. As long as she acts sensibly and doesn't receive any shocks, she'll go on forever. She wouldn't give in to the flu at first, you see. Refused to go to bed even though she had a high temperature. Her housekeeper got worried, phoned the doctor, and that's when the doctor contacted me. I'm going back over there tomorrow or Saturday, and I'm bringing her with me when I return on Sunday. She'll stay at the Hall until after New Year if I have my way.'

The rest of their short journey continued without conversation until Bryce drew up outside the shop and said, 'That announcement has done some good. You've a shop full of customers. Let's give them something to make their visit worthwhile.'

9

Before Flora realised what Bryce meant, he'd lowered his face to hers and was kissing her with a tenderness she wanted to sink into. She responded with a warmth that surprised her and, she thought, surprised Bryce too.

They were forced to end this special moment between them when there was a loud tooting noise from behind. Reluctantly moving away, Flora glanced over her shoulder. 'It's a flower delivery from Holland,' she said, making to open the car door.

Bryce leant across her and with a heart-turning smile said, 'The newspaper was right about no need for mistletoe. I'll see you this evening, Flora.'

Flustered, she got out of the car as fast as she could. Perhaps Bryce was flustered, too, because he drove off quickly, and she found herself staring at an empty space. Then she became aware of the driver of the Dutch vehicle walking towards her grinning all over his face, and she felt herself blushing. But at least she had some excuse for not going into the shop right away and having to put up with the customers teasing her; she could check the delivery first then take the boxes in the back way to the preparation room. That didn't take long, though, and anyway it wasn't fair to leave Pippa to cope on her own when it was so busy. Taking a deep breath, she went through into the shop.

True, there were a few knowing glances and a bit of teasing. Pippa's chuckles didn't help either, but it was all so good-natured and friendly that Flora's embarrassment vanished and she found herself responding light-heartedly to the banter.

★ ★ ★

However, once on her own again and driving home to get changed before going for her dress fitting, Flora dropped her light-hearted act. She was having great difficulty in coming to terms with her feelings. Earlier on she'd thought Bryce had told the family about their fake engagement and had wondered why she didn't feel glad that the need for pretence was over. Now, far from the family knowing that it hadn't been for real, the need for pretence was stronger than ever.

'And I feel more depressed than ever,' she muttered. 'Even the fact that Bryce hadn't invited Jilly Joy round last Sunday hasn't made me feel any better.'

Of course, deep down she knew why she felt depressed, but didn't want to admit it. Didn't want to admit that not only was she still a hundred percent attracted to Bryce, but she was and always had been in love with him. He could be cold, cynical, arrogant, tormenting, loving, kind, tender and loyal. He was all she'd ever want, ever need;

but acknowledging that would hurt too much.

Ignoring the scenery, for she knew the poignancy of its winter splendour would cut into her like a sharp knife, she kept her eyes straight ahead and wondered who had spoken to the newspaper and put her in this unenviable position. It seemed like it had to have been Val — but that didn't add up to the Val she knew. She couldn't imagine her friend finding the time or having the inclination to do that, especially while Mrs Torman was so ill. Bryce had said it was only yesterday the danger of pneumonia had passed. That didn't leave enough time for Val to contact the newspaper offices.

Whoever had done it didn't make any difference. She and Bryce would have to act like an engaged couple in public as well as in front of the family. Flora wasn't sure how she'd be able to bear that.

★   ★   ★

Inspiration struck a couple of hours later when she was standing in front of a mirror wearing her bridesmaid dress. A few months ago she'd been approached by a prosperous hotelier and property owner to set up a chain of flower boutiques in his hotel foyers and the reception areas of prestigious business and residential apartments. Not only in the UK but in Belgium and Holland, too. At the time, although the challenge had appealed, the idea of being away from home for long stretches of time hadn't. Now, though, it could save her sanity. True, there'd still be the Christmas party and Val's wedding to get through . . .

Flora let out a deep sigh which earned an anxious look from the couturiere. 'Don't worry. Just a little tuck here at the waist and it will be perfect. See, like this.' Deft fingers nipped and pinned.

Flora smiled. 'It's lovely,' she praised. Though in all honesty, her thoughts were far away from the dress. It could have been a sack for all the impression it was making. However, her words seemed to please the couturiere, for she nodded in a satisfied manner before helping Flora out of the soft velvet folds.

Normally, Flora would have lingered a while to examine the new materials and fabric designs tastefully displayed around the walls of the sample room. The riot of colours intrigued her and, more often than not, her browsing produced an idea for an unusual floral arrangement. Today, though, she needed time and space to think of other things. Having known in advance of her dress fitting, she'd already told her shop managers she'd be unavailable this afternoon, so she decided to spend a couple of hours walking round the delightful country town.

Mentioning this to the couturiere, she was given advice as to what she must see and also directions to the best place to procure afternoon tea. After laughingly promising she'd be sure to try the gingerbread for which this Derbyshire Dales area was famous, Flora buttoned her cosy swing coat and made her way down the steep stairs to the front door.

Two minutes later, outside the establishment that was housed in a side street a short distance from the town centre, Flora was feverishly scrabbling in her large shoulder-bag as she stared at the empty space where she'd parked the Suzuki. Surely she hadn't left her keys in the ignition? True, she'd been preoccupied, her mind focused on what she'd have to endure over the next couple of weeks; but she just couldn't have neglected to secure her car.

No. she hadn't. Her fingers fastened around her keyring in its usual place — a narrow pocket inside her bag. So where was her car? Parking was permitted here; it couldn't have been towed away. She turned ready to run back inside and phone the police station and found herself enveloped in a strong pair of arms.

'Bryce.' She'd known who it was immediately she'd felt his touch; hadn't needed to look up into his face. Now, however, she did. 'What are you doing here, and where's my car?' That he was responsible for its disappearance she had no doubt. After all it had been his advice, given long ago when she'd bought her very first car, that she should always keep a spare ignition key taped securely underneath.

He gave a lopsided smile and raised an eyebrow; Flora felt her heart pounding but somehow couldn't convince herself that it was anger causing the erratic thumping. 'I knew you were coming here for your dress fitting,' he said smoothly. 'So I brought Val with me in my car. It's parked round the corner. She's er . . . borrowed your car and will return it to you this evening. Meanwhile . . . ' He turned her round, at the same time linking one hand through her arm and pulling her close into the side of his body.

To anyone looking on, it would have seemed like an affectionate gesture. To Flora, it felt as though there were a band of heat around her arm; she could feel it through the thick wool of her coat, so sensitive was her body to his touch. Thoughts spun dizzily through her mind as she tried to fight the physical sensations generated by his proximity.

She heard his voice, but his words didn't register as he said, 'Meanwhile, you and I have someone to see.'

He was walking now, and there was no other choice than to walk with him, unless she wanted to be dragged along. For, through the maelstrom raging inside her, Flora had seen and recognised the look of determination in his dark-brown eyes when they'd flickered over her face. Strangely, for a moment she was actually enjoying her own submissiveness; relishing the feeling of power he had over her. *Maybe it's because I've made up my mind to go away after New Year,* she mused. *I've so little time left to be with him that I'll accept any crumbs he offers. Make memories to take with me.*

For she knew she would take up the offer of setting up a chain of flower boutiques; it was the only thing she could do. As she lengthened her stride to keep up with him, his words worked their way up into her sluggish brain and she snapped to life. 'What do you mean we have someone to see? *I've* got places to see, things to do. I don't want to — '

'And I don't want to argue, Flora,' he stated. 'We'll come in for a lot of attention this evening at Val's wedding rehearsal: the vicar, the choirboys, the other bridesmaids, the flower girls, page boys. There's no way we're attending unless you're wearing an engagement ring. We're going to buy you one.'

Flora stopped dead in her tracks and glared at him. 'I don't want an engagement ring.' To her dismay, her words hadn't come out firm and strong as she'd meant them to. Her voice had actually wobbled. Panic-stricken, she lowered her head and gazed unseeingly at the pavement. For finally she was listening to her heart — the that which was telling her she loved Bryce with her whole being. To wear his ring that to everyone else would be a declaration of shared love and intention to many — to wear such a token when it was meaning-less — would hurt way too much.

Heavens, if she wasn't careful, if she didn't pull herself together, she wouldn't be able to deal with this emotional vul-nerability that had surfaced and Bryce would see her love for him. She couldn't let that happen. As a teenager she'd shown him her love and he'd rejected both it and her. She couldn't face his rejection again.

A distressed whimper rose inside her and threatened to emerge. She bit hard on her lip to prevent it. But a strangled gasp escaped, and it seemed Bryce had heard it. Firm but gentle fingers lifted her chin and, almost against her will, she looked into his eyes. They were like dark, deep pools pulling at her very soul and as he spoke. 'Please, Flora, we have to do it.' His voice was raw with emotion.

She felt as though she was drowning

in a sea of heartbreak as she slowly nodded her head and allowed him to guide her to his car.

10

Once in the Ferrari, Bryce didn't start up straight away. Turning to face her, he said in a voice now devoid of all emotion, 'You said you had places to go. If you've a business appointment ... ?' He left the question hanging in the air.

If I had a business appointment I'd have cancelled it if we'd been going to choose a ring for a real engagement, Flora thought painfully. Then she wondered if she should lie and say she had got one and she couldn't spare time to go and choose a ring, even though she'd agreed by nodding her head. But a look of impatience crossed his face and she answered hurriedly, 'No, not a business appointment. I was going to do a spot of sight-seeing, that's all. Look at the inn with two signs — the Clergy Widows' Alms-houses.

Forty-three craftsmen were involved in the building of them . . . ' She knew she'd sound like a guidebook if she didn't stop, but if she stopped she'd start hurting more. 'I wanted to see the house where the famous Doctor Johnson used to stay, and the church with the spire known as the Pride of the Peak.' His eyebrows were drawn together, his fingers tapping on the steering wheel. She shrugged her shoulders and concluded, 'Nothing important . . . ' Letting her words tail off, she reached for her seat belt.

'Whereas an engagement ring is important, though neither of us thought that social nicety would be necessary when we got caught up in this charade.'

'Social nicety.' Unintentionally she'd repeated the words aloud — though her repetition held a bitter anguish.

'It's the only way to look at it.' He sounded cold, impersonal almost, and he wasn't looking at her. The low purr indicated that he'd started the car, though she hadn't noticed his hand moving to the ignition. She glanced sideways at him, but he was checking the mirror prior to pulling out.

'I'm sorry you find the thought of wearing an engagement ring so distasteful,' he added in the same cold tones.

He was putting her emotional state down to distaste, Flora realised in amazement. When in reality . . . She opened her mouth, then firmly closed it. There was no way to explain why she didn't want to wear a ring without giving away her true feelings for him.

To her relief, it wasn't long before the Pride of the Peak came into view. 'Oh, look,' she said brightly. 'Slow down a bit, there's the church I wanted to see. What a magnificent spire. I believe it's two hundred and twelve feet high and pierced with dormer lights.'

That would show him, she thought, proud of her insouciant manner. Turning to look out of the back window, she continued, 'You've heard the song by Tom Moore, 'Those Evening Bells'? It was the pealing of

185

this church's bells that inspired him.'

'He also wrote 'The Last Rose of Summer', the song used in *Martha*, that comic opera,' said Bryce.

Drat him. His insouciance had topped hers; he was playing her at her own game by acting as though they were tourists on a day trip. Well, she wouldn't give him any more ammunition. She'd take refuge in silence. He couldn't converse on his own. She swivelled back round and stared straight ahead.

* * *

Soon the silence was almost unbearable. She wouldn't give in, though. She resorted to an old childhood game — trying to spot consecutive numbers from one to nine on car number plates.

She thought she heard a smothered laugh and turned her head. That was a mistake; he was changing gear and her eyes were drawn to the way the fabric of his trousers pulled against the muscles in his thighs. Hastily she averted her gaze, only to find it falling on his hands resting on the steering wheel.

The hands that would soon be touching hers, for she knew without any doubt that Bryce 'for appearances' sake' would slip any ring they chose onto her finger himself. She was filled with an aching need to reach out and touch him. Aching for the impossible, too, she admitted. She wanted him to love her. How had that happened? How had she allowed these feelings to take her over again?

'We're almost there.' His voice was a welcome intrusion into her turbulent thoughts. 'Perhaps you should powder your face,' he continued. 'You look rather — '

'If you don't like the way I look, you've only yourself to blame,' Flora told him. 'First you steal my car, and then you coerce me into coming to a jeweller's. How the — '

'On the contrary.' It was his turn to interrupt now. 'I quite like the way you look, and the jeweller will put your rosy

187

cheeks and sparkling eyes down to something entirely different to temper.'

How right the jeweller will be, Flora admitted to herself, delving into her shoulder-bag to find her powder compact. Then wishing she hadn't. Bryce had bought her the compact for her sixteenth birthday. How silly she'd been to keep it all these years. And what would he think if he recognised it?

However, after neatly reversing the car into a convenient parking space, he showed no sign of doing so as he coolly watched her dabbing a light film of powder over her heated cheeks. *Why should he remember that he gave it to me?* Flora thought sourly. He must have bought so many things for so many women over the years. Had he bought them jewellery from the jeweller's they were about to visit? Or, worse still, how many of his women had he taken with him to the jeweller's?

'You'll like Jervis,' Bryce assured her as they walked towards a row of old-fashioned-looking shops. 'He's an old family friend. Dad bought Mother's engagement ring here.'

To Flora's surprise, Bryce didn't attempt to open the shop door. Instead he placed his finger on an ancient bell at the side of the door. 'Early-closing day,' he explained. 'But Jervis is expecting us.'

* * *

Flora knew she'd never forget the heart-rending poignancy of the time spent with the kindly old jeweller. He'd greeted them with old-fashioned courtesy, his respect and fondness for Bryce written plainly on his lined face as he'd insisted on then partaking of sherry and ratafia biscuits before looking at engagement rings.

And Bryce played his part to perfection, treating her with such gentle tenderness that even she almost felt as though his feelings for her were genuine. When Jervis finally brought a tray of rings for their inspection, Bryce unerringly picked the one that Flora would have chosen if all this had been real.

But it isn't real, she anguished, tears smarting behind her eyelids as Bryce took her hand in his and slipped an antique ring of amethyst and pearls onto her finger.

'It could have been made for you . . . for us,' he said huskily, raising her hand to his lips and kissing it.

The tears escaped then, trickling silently down her cheeks.

'It's lucky for tears of happiness to fall upon the engagement ring chosen together with love,' Jervis informed her before placing a gentle kiss on her cheek. Then, turning to Bryce, he said, 'It's an old Roman belief that an artery goes straight to the heart from the third finger on the left hand. By placing the ring there, you'll live in her heart forever. I wish you both all the happiness in the world.'

★ ★ ★

Flora had no recollection of saying goodbye to Jervis — or of walking with Bryce to the car, getting in it and setting off. No recollection of anything other than the waves of pain still sweeping through her.

Now she emerged from that, feeling numb and cold, as Bryce spoke sharply. 'Flora. I said we're here.' Then she heard him groan and murmur something incomprehensible; was vaguely aware of him getting out of the car.

Then the passenger door opened, he unfastened her seat-belt, put his hand under her elbow and guided her out of the car. They were halfway up the stone steps before it registered that Bryce had brought her to his home. Like a zombie, she followed him in through the front door, through the hall and in to the lounge.

'Flora.' He turned and took a step towards her, and she found herself in his arms. He held her close; she could feel the heat from his body warming the coldness of hers. She thought she felt his lips brushing across her bowed head, thought she felt him tremble. She wanted to stay here forever, safe and secure in this newfound paradise.

'Flora . . . ' He said again. Then, with a muttered curse, he was releasing her; and the protest that sprang to her lips died as her eyes focused on Hector standing in the open doorway.

Shortly, Flora was to be grateful for Hector's intrusion — she'd been close to sobbing out her true feelings against Bryce's comforting chest. At the time, though, she resented it and wished fervently that either she or Bryce had thought to secure the front door.

'I've come to explain about precipitating things,' Hector said. 'The announcement in today's local rag,' he added, presumably registering neither his nephew nor Flora knew what he was talking about.

Hell's bells, the announcement — the cause of all this . . . this . . . Flora shook her head. Was it really only this morning? She'd lost all sense of time. But Hector was still talking; she made herself concentrate on his words.

' . . . handing in my weekly column to the editor,' he was saying. 'There staring up at me was a page of nonsense about that Jilly Joy.' His voice hardened and he glared at his nephew. 'It was making out she was going to marry you, Bryce. I'm fed up with the Torman name being thrown into ridicule, I had to stop the speculation so I told the editor it was a load of rubbish and you were engaged to Flora.'

Hector shook his head. 'I thought that would stop them from printing the Jilly Joy article. I had no idea they'd still run it and even less idea they'd use it to publicise your engagement.'

'So, seeing as they did . . . ' Bryce reached for Flora's left hand and held it towards his uncle.

'That isn't your aunt's ring, Bryce, the one she bequeathed to you for your future wife.'

Flora felt Bryce stiffen. He let go of her hand, and for the briefest moment there was an almost tangible tension in the air; but it evaporated when Bryce replied coolly, 'No, I'm sorry, Uncle. I didn't think it would suit Flora.'

He means I wouldn't suit it, Flora thought. *I'm still not good enough for the great Bryce Torman, even in a pretend engagement.*

'So I may have inadvertently pushed the pair of you into speeding things up, but no real harm done, eh?'

'No harm at all, Uncle Hector,' Bryce agreed smoothly, turning to smile at Flora. 'Isn't that so, sweetheart?'

Still anguishing about Bryce not thinking her good enough to wear his aunt's ring, she glared at him without replying.

'At least now,' Bryce said into the uncomfortable silence, 'I'll be able to keep an eye on Jilly for her parents without causing malicious gossip.'

Anger came to Flora's rescue, restoring her self-respect. After telling her she wouldn't be able to see Rupert, he'd calmly announced his intention of 'keeping an eye on Jilly'.

And to think, Flora fumed, *if Hector hadn't arrived when he did, I'd probably have told Bryce I'm in love with him for real. Thought I was*, she corrected, for her heart's pendulum had swung firmly back to contempt for both him and herself.

So when Hector commented that Flora must be a very trusting person if she didn't mind Bryce keeping an eye on Jilly Joy, Flora replied sweetly, 'Oh, Bryce knows how much I trust him — don't you, darling?' She hoped the look she'd shot him made her meaning more than clear. Pride to the fore, she added, 'Now I must go and find Mother to show her my ring. I'll have tea with her, and then we can drive to the wedding rehearsal in her car, seeing as Val has got mine. I'll see you both there.'

Bryce stretched out an arm to detain her. 'I thought we'd be having tea here. I asked Jemima to make your favourite cake.'

'I hope you aren't thinking of

purloining my housekeeper when you get married,' Hector said.

'No fear of that,' Flora told him, shooting another meaningful glance at Bryce. 'Do apologise to Jemima for my not staying for tea, but I'm sure she'll understand. Mother is expecting me and we both agree — don't we, Bryce? — that mothers shouldn't be upset.'

After removing Bryce's hand from her arm, Fiona flashed the two men a smile and, head held high, walked out.

* * *

Flora laughed as three anxious faces turned towards her. She'd had a hectic day and was still fired up by adrenalin. Yesterday and its happenings — including the wedding rehearsal, where with Bryce at her side she'd had to accept and smile through congratulations on their engagement — was for now a niggling memory at the back of her mind.

'I asked you here this evening to

impart what I hope you'll feel is good news,' she told Justin, Sue and Pippa.

Sue looked at her alertly. 'I hope that means you aren't selling the flower boutiques when you get married.'

'Good grief,' Flora said, 'I'm sorry — I never realised you might imagine that was the reason I'd invited you round.' She saw all three visibly relax now and went on to explain how she was thinking of accepting the offer made by a businessman to set up a chain of flower boutiques in reception areas of his luxury hotels and other prestigious premises both here and abroad.

'So you'd be spreading your wings before settling down to married life,' said Justin.

Flora nodded and, after assurances from all three of them that they'd be willing to take on extra responsibilities and train new staff if necessary, she discussed her plans and ideas in more detail.

The evening sped past and by the

time it was over, Flora was convinced that accepting the offer would be the right thing to do. *Bryce, she thought, will be so relieved I'll not be around so much and will back me to the hilt when we tell our mothers and his uncle. We can say it's something I want to do while there's still time. Like Justin, they'll think I mean before settling down to marriage. And it'll be so much easier after a couple of months to explain there won't be any marriage. We can say that my absence caused us to drift apart.*

So all she had to do first, she mused as she got ready for bed, was to get through the rest of December. 'And then a week or so after that it'll be goodbye to this fiasco and Bryce Torman,' she muttered as she removed the amethyst and pearl engagement ring from her finger and placed it on her bedside cabinet.

But the buzz of adrenalin that had kept her buoyed up for a good few hours seemed to have disappeared down the plughole with the bathwater, because by the time she was in bed, that bruised and vulnerable feeling ate into her again. She knew why: it was that darned ring glowing softly in the light from her bedside lamp. If only it could have really meant something. *But, no, it's another ring — the one his aunt left him. Bryce will give to the one he loves.*

Why couldn't her love her? Why couldn't she stop loving him? Because no matter what he did or said, and no matter how she despised him at times — although her love for him burnt away to ashes at times — there was always one ember waiting to be fanned back into life.

How melodramatic, she mocked herself angrily and thumped her pillow. It was up to her to put out that ember for good. An almost impossible task until she'd be able to get away from him. And that certainly wouldn't be happening this weekend, would it?

When Bryce was saying goodnight

after Val's wedding rehearsal, sheer bravado had made Flora agree to his suggestion of driving to his mother's with him on Saturday afternoon. Staying the night and returning on Sunday.

Today, she'd managed not to think of that. Talking on the phone to Gurth Godwin, the hotelier, who seemed delighted to hear she would now seriously consider his business proposal; jotting down a few outline plans in between the normal day-today running of the three flower boutiques; and then having her three main employees round to her flat had kept her mind occupied. And it was that which she should be thinking of now, not Bryce. But at least she'd be able to tell him about her future plans tomorrow afternoon on the way to his mother's.

'But,' she whispered to 'His Patchiness', her old, battered teddy bear she'd brought to bed for comfort, 'I mustn't let the relief he's sure to show when he hears them hurt me.'

★ ★ ★

In the morning when she reluctantly got out of bed, Flora glanced in the mirror and was horrified by her pallor and the dark circles under her eyes. It was only to be expected really, with all that had happened over the last few days. And the thought of Bryce picking her up at five o'clock wasn't helping, either. But before that, she was visiting a client in Yorkshire to firm up on the arrangements for a children's party with an indoor 'Enchanted Forest' theme. If she didn't do something about her appearance, she'd be cast as the witch of the forest.

Twenty minutes later, she was jogging around the park hoping the crispy, frosty weather would bring colour to her cheeks and a sparkle to her eyes. Her steady, rhythmic movements soothed her, and the frozen cobwebs stretched across the bushes gave her a new idea to incorporate into her Enchanted Forest design. So the jog did her good in more ways than one, and now she was looking forward to driving to Yorkshire to discuss plans with Debra and James Woodford and their four children.

11

Flora had a natural rapport with children and was always ready to listen to their ideas of what they wanted in any set she designed for their parties. And today, the four young Woodfords were full of ideas.

'We want the way into the forest to be all dark and gloomy,' explained Sophie, the eldest. 'Then all of a sudden there'll be a clearing where we find Father Christmas. Uncle Speckles is going to be Father Christmas.'

'Uncle Speck's going to try on his outfit today,' said one of the boys.

Flora wondered if the uncle wore specs or had freckles but thought it better not to ask.

'Fairy lights will flash on . . . ' Sophie continued. 'Daddy's doing the lights . . . and Father Christmas will be inside a hollow tree trunk.'

'*Wiv* a reindeer,' lisped three-year-old Amelia.

Sophie smiled at her. 'Yes, with a reindeer. Uncle Speckles has brought some tree trunks and logs and weird-shaped branches from his place, Flora. He didn't cut anything down especially; the trees came down in a storm.

'Anyway, Oliver and William, sometimes known as 'Tree' and 'Helmet' because that's what their names mean . . . ' Sophie pointed to her brothers one at a time. ' . . . thought maybe you could make a reindeer from logs and branches.'

'Could you, d'you think?' asked William.

'Dad and Uncle Speck are right now hollowing out a trunk where Father Christmas will sit with his reindeer,' Oliver added.

'I expect I could,' Flora replied.

'*Wiv* antlers and a red nose?' said Amelia.

Reaching for her sketchpad and pencil, Flora began to draw. 'How about something like this? See, if your uncle's brought some nice big logs we could hollow one out for the reindeer's body and hide presents there. Maybe your dad can fix a red light to the nose and make it flash on and off when Father Christmas pulls a present out of the reindeer's tummy.'

Flora knew James Woodford was a stage lighting director at one of the big theatres — in fact, Flora had first met him and his wife when she'd designed a floral set for a play at his theatre. He'd be more than capable of giving the reindeer a flashing nose.

'That's so cool,' breathed Sophie. 'Look, Mum,' she added as Debra came into the room, 'Flora's sketched a brilliant idea.'

'Can we take this to show Dad and Uncle Speck?' Oliver asked Flora.

'If your mum says it's all right,' Flora told him.

'Mum says that's fine.' Smiling, Debra shooed the four of them out of the room.

'Now we'll have a coffee, Flora, and we can talk over your plans for the enchanted forest in peace. I hope the children's ideas haven't interfered too much with yours?'

'Not at all. Though I hadn't quite planned for Father Christmas to be inside a tree trunk with a reindeer. I hope their uncle knows that part of it.'

Debra laughed. 'He does. He's actually an honorary uncle; James and I have known him years and he adores the children. It's about time he settled down and produced a few of his own. He'd be a marvellous father. James and I were both 'onlies'; that's why we decided to have a large family. You obviously like children, Flora. Are you planning on a large family when you get married? I'm sorry, maybe I shouldn't have asked that but I couldn't help noticing your gorgeous engagement ring. You weren't wearing it last time you came, were you?'

Flora was saved from answering by the reappearance of the children asking her to come to the room where the party would be held. 'Just wait until you see what Dad and Uncle Speckles have done! It's fantastic. But Amelia's worried about her reindeer. She doesn't believe you can turn logs and branches into one.'

'But Father Christmas knows a magic spell that will help,' said Amelia.

'Oh, that's all right then,' laughed Flora, lifting Amelia up. 'Let's sing the reindeer song,' she suggested. 'That will help, too.'

Singing and laughing, they made their way down the hall to the large, long room, which had been cleared of all furniture and carpeting in readiness for the party next week. At the far end stood a massive hollow tree trunk — carried in through the French windows, Flora guessed. She was still singing along with Amelia as they reached the tree trunk with Father Christmas in full regalia inside it.

'Father Christmas, tell Flora about the magic spell to help the logs and branches turn into a reindeer,' Amelia shouted, nearly deafening Flora in the process.

Father Christmas beckoned. Still carrying Amelia, Flora laughingly obeyed his summons. He held out his arms for Amelia and whispered in her ear.

'Your whiskers and big fluffy beard are tickly,' she protested. Then she smacked a wet kiss on his cheek and he put her down.

'Flora, you've got to kiss him now. He says that's the magic spell. Kisses.'

Entering into the spirit of things, Flora moved forward to kiss the cheek held towards her. But her lips didn't end up on Father Christmas's cheek. Instead, his mouth touched hers and gentle lips delicately explored hers.

Lips she knew.

12

Flora gasped her shock against those warm lips and felt her body tremble as the kiss lengthened gloriously.

Giggles from the children broke the spell and Flora hastily backed away, guessing her face would be as red as the traditional Santa costume.

'Hello, darling. Surprised to see me?'

'Flora!' Debra said. 'I'd no idea it was Bryce you're engaged to. Why didn't you tell me? I mean . . . ' She clapped a hand to her mouth and stared in comical dismay at Flora.

'It is, isn't it? I mean, you couldn't have kissed him like that if you weren't.'

'Debs,' warned her husband, 'you're going from bad to worse.'

Flora waited in vain for Bryce to say something, but he stayed annoyingly silent though his eyes showed his amusement.

'I'd no idea 'Uncle Speckles' was Bryce,' returned Flora at last, not really answering Debra's question and hoping nobody would notice the shakiness of her voice. 'How could I have?'

'I told you how we sometimes call Oliver and William 'Tree' and 'Helmet' because that's what their names mean,' Sophie interrupted. 'Well, the name Bryce means 'speckled', and me, my sister and brothers like calling him Uncle Speckles or Speck more than Uncle Bryce.'

'But why didn't *you* tell us you were engaged to Flora, Bryce, when you knew she was coming here this morning?' Debra demanded.

'You never actually said her name. So until a few minutes ago, I'd no idea the party planner and designer you'd booked was my fiancée.' Bryce shrugged. 'I'm aware of how well-known she is for her floral designs, of course, but I didn't realise her reputation had spread this far. We are seventy miles or so away from home. James and I were at agricultural college together,' he explained, putting an arm around Flora's shoulders. 'But James decided farming wasn't for him and went into the theatre instead.'

'That's where Debra and I met Flora,' put in James. 'Doing a floral set for a play. We liked her ideas so much we booked her for this party.'

'You know when we were talking in the kitchen, Flora, I was thinking what a shame it was you were engaged,' confided Debra. 'I knew you'd be perfect for Bryce, you see. And all the time it was him. It's fantastic. Now, what I want to know — '

'I want a reindeer,' Amelia interrupted, tugging at Bryce's red coat. 'Please, Uncle Speckles, we've done the magic spell.'

'We sure have, sweetheart,' agreed Bryce, winking outrageously at Flora, who knew she'd blushed again as she thought about that spell. 'Now,' Bryce continued, 'we'll make the best reindeer you've ever seen. You are going to help us, aren't you, *Floradorable*?'

Flora cringed at the silly name he'd

clearly made up to sound like a loving fiancé. Luckily before she could snap a reply, Debra spoke.

'Flora, you must stay for lunch,' she commanded. 'We're having a boat barbecue on our longboat. It's moored at the bottom of the garden. You probably noticed that the canal goes straight past us. Bryce is cooking; barbecues are one of his specialities. Oh.' She laughed. 'You'll know that already, Flora.'

'Bonfire Nights on the estate,' Bryce reminded her. 'I was always chief sausage cook then.'

'I remember they were always black and shrivelled to nothing. Val and I used to give ours to that crazy dog you had. What was his name, Benzo?'

'No, Flora vegetable spread,' taunted Bryce, 'it was Bonzo.' He howled in anguish as Flora retaliated by neatly whisking his white beard off. 'You've pulled half my skin away with it.'

'Want a reindeer,' said the persistent Amelia, glaring reproachfully at Bryce.

'All right, just let me get out of this outfit and we'll make Rudolph.'

'I'll leave you lot to it and go and marinate some extra steaks,' said Debra, hurrying away.

Flora didn't know whether to be glad or sorry. Debra's friendly chatter could be embarrassing, but it acted as a buffer between herself and Bryce. She wasn't too sure about the wisdom of staying for lunch, either, but couldn't see a way out of it.

*   *   *

Driving home, after promising Bryce she'd be ready for six o'clock — later than they'd first intended leaving to go to his mother's — Flora played over the time she'd spent with the Woodfords and Bryce. She'd seen a new side to Bryce today. Debra had been quite right when she'd said that he would make a marvellous father. Of course, now she thought about it, she'd always been aware of his gentleness and empathy with the

213

estate workers' children, but she'd never visualised him as a natural family man. For that was what he was, there was no doubt about it.

Why then had he never married? He'd certainly had plenty of opportunities. Surely he must have met someone suitable. All right, he acted the playboy, and many of his girlfriends had been the glamourous model-girl types who probably wouldn't fit into his life at Torman Hall. But what about that brunette he had disappeared with at the Christmas party last year — the daughter of a neighbouring landowner? With her similar background, she'd be ideal.

'But I never could understand him,' she muttered. 'And I understand myself even less.' For no matter how hard she tried, she couldn't dispel the yearning that had come over her when she and Bryce were making the reindeer with the four Woodford children. The yearning to bear his children, a physical ache that had deepened when they'd taken

Amelia up to her bedroom and settled her down for an afternoon nap. Obeying the little one's sleepy command, they'd sat together on her bed and sang the reindeer song for her. Then she'd watched Bryce bend over the sleeping child and gently kiss her forehead . . .

Flora gave a deep sigh. Here she was, back at square one . . . loving him, wanting him, needing him. Crying for the moon.

* * *

'What are you doing, crying for the moon?'

Flora nearly jumped out of her skin at the sound of Bryce's voice echoing the very phrase she'd used to herself a couple of hours ago.

At a few minutes to six, she'd decided to wait outside for Bryce to arrive. For some inexplicable reason she hadn't wanted him to come up to fetch her. But as she'd stood staring up at the full moon, hauntingly beautiful in the navy-blue starlit sky, the reason had become clear. It was because the last time they'd been together in her flat, eating Mario's pasta, they'd shared happy memories.

Seeing him in the flat now, while still feeling an overpowering longing for him — a longing for what could never be — would have brought back that memory of the togetherness they'd shared then. For, apart from when they'd been in his car on their way to somewhere, the previous Saturday was about the only time recently they'd spent alone, just the two them.

True, they'd be alone together in a few minutes, but again they'd be in his car; and at the end of their journey, his mother would be there. And just as Flora was wishing that wasn't so and it could be just the two of them for the rest of the weekend, Bryce arrived and asked her that question. An apt one that tore her very soul to pieces. For she *was* still 'crying for the moon'; probably hadn't stopped doing so since that long-ago night when Bryce had made it obvious an estate worker's daughter wouldn't be suitable for the heir to Torman Hall.

'You've no right sneaking up on me like that, Bryce,' she said now, inwardly cursing the fact that shock and hurt made her voice harsh — the harshness entirely at odds with the beauty of the evening.

'Excuse me for breathing,' he drawled sarcastically, his voice and face as cold as the chill in the air. 'I didn't mean to make you jump,' he continued, moving to stand in front of her, his tone more gentle now, and his breath swirling towards her. 'I didn't realise you hadn't seen me. Presumably you were expecting me . . .' He pointed to the overnight case by her feet. ' . . . Unless of course you were planning on spending this evening and tomorrow with someone else?'

'I wish I *was* spending the weekend with someone else.' It was a lie, but she had to protect herself from showing her true feelings. She answered the first question then: 'Of course I was expecting you. On four wheels, not on soundless feet.'

'I left my wheels outside the gates. It seemed silly to bring them in and go to all the trouble of turning them straight round.'

Was he making fun of her? Had she imagined hidden laughter? she wondered, glancing up at him. His expression was deadpan; and as he stared back at her, the light from the moon seemed to dance over him, casting an almost eerie sheen on his dark hair and enhancing the planes and angles of his face.

She caught her breath; and as anger died and pain returned, she took a step back. *Oh, Bryce, why has it got to be like this between us?* she mourned silently.

'You know, the one thing I used to admire about you in the old days, Flora, was your willingness to laugh at the ridiculous things you said in anger. You seem to have completely lost that ability.'

'Maybe 'in the old days' *you* had the

ability to make me laugh,' she retorted. 'Or maybe I just save my laughter for someone who's worth it.'

'Touché. Now we've evened the score, shall we go?'

'You make it sound as though I've a choice,' she muttered childishly, bending down to pick up her overnight case.

Bryce reached for it at the same time. Their fingers brushed and she felt as though she'd received an electric shock. Her fingers tightened, as if by clenching them around the handle she could prevent the currents from entering her body.

Clearly, completely misreading her action, Bryce tightened his own grip on the handle, tugging at the case, obviously determined he'd win the right to carry it. Flora tugged back, felt her feet slipping from under her, and grabbed Bryce's arm with her free hand, her unexpected movement catching him off balance. They fell to the ground together, letting go of the case. It skidded away, the impact causing it to open and spill out its contents, which brought a hysterical giggle from Flora.

'So I've lost the ability to make you laugh, have I?' challenged Bryce a couple of seconds later, turning his body and kneeling over her, pushing his laughing face against hers.

Flora's giggles turned to laughter as, over Bryce's shoulder, she glimpsed the stunned faces of a group of carol singers standing as though frozen to the spot, a lantern on a pole illuminating the belongings from her case — especially, it seemed, her crazily striped long woollen socks.

'If they sing 'While Shepherds Watched Their Flocks',' she gasped, remembering how as youngsters they'd changed the last three words to 'washed their socks',' I think I'll die of laughter.'

'What are you talking about? Did you hit your head when you fell?'

Flora shook her head, lifted her hands to his face and turned it towards their audience and the clothes from her case.

'Oh, I see what you mean.' He chuckled, helping her to her feet. 'I'd better say something to reassure the singers, hadn't I? Shall we invite them into your flat for a drink? I'll take them up and put the kettle on while you rescue your belongings.'

Twenty minutes later, as the carol singers drank hot chocolate and ate shortbread biscuits — Flora had opened the tin she'd bought to take to Bryce's mother's — Bryce pulled her to one side and said, 'Have you still got your accordion?'

'Of course I have.' Her mind went winging back to the barn dances they had on the estate at harvest time. She'd often perched on the seat of the tractor, playing tunes for the dances.

'How about giving it an airing? Let's join the carollers on their merry round of the town.'

'What about your mother?' she reminded him wistfully. 'She's expecting us.'

'I phoned her while you were

handing out the good cheer, just to warn her we'd be late. However, she's got a couple of surprise visitors — an old school friend and her daughter who moved away to live in Australia years ago. Mother hinted that if we arrived tomorrow instead of this evening, her friends could stay the night instead of booking in at the local hotel. I had a word with Marjorie, the old school friend, and she promised to watch that Mother didn't over-do things. I said we'd join them in the morning for a late breakfast. So I thought . . . ?'

'You thought we'd go carol-singing. It's a lovely idea, Bryce. I'll go and get Squeeze.' She laughed at his raised brow. 'Squeeze-box . . . Accordion.'

'Squeeze,' he muttered in disgust. 'Just don't suggest bringing His Patchiness,' he implored, and Flora stuck her tongue out at him before hurrying away to fetch the accordion.

It wasn't long before they made their way back outside and contentment filled Flora as she and Bryce became part of the happy throng raising their voices in song . . .

★ ★ ★

'We must have walked miles. I don't know which muscles are protesting the most, the ones in my legs or the ones in my arms.' Back in her flat, after putting a match to the ready-laid fire, Flora sunk on to the sofa with a grateful sigh. 'It's years since I played Squeeze.'

'You should have let me have a turn of playing.'

Flora shook her head.

'Hey, I'm not that bad.'

'Oh, yes you are,' she returned, pantomime style. 'I remember — '

'I remember you used to like the scrambled eggs I sometimes made for you and Val. Have you got eggs? If so, I'll be head cook again. I don't know about you, but singing has given me an appetite.'

'I can't judge what's getting to me the most, aching muscles or my hunger,' said Flora.

223

'Go and have a bath if you like and soothe those aches while I go and do the food.'

'I do like. A bath is exactly what my body needs.' She walked towards the door. 'There's bacon and mushrooms in the fridge,' she said over her shoulder. 'No point in half-doing things.'

'No point at all.' Bryce's voice sounded strangely husky, but Flora put it down to all the singing.

A few minutes later, exotically perfumed bath foam was bubbling delicately over her weary body as she lay back in the bath lost in thought. Flora was determined nothing would mar the rest of their evening together.

Accepting the fact that Bryce would never return her love, even though the acceptance hurt deeply, she made up her mind to nurture their fragile friendship. It was less than she wanted, but better than being at loggerheads.

'A lot less than I want,' she murmured, stroking the ring on her finger.

The ring. She'd forgotten to remove it before getting into the bath. Standing up, she took it off and stretched across to place it on the shelf of the mirror above the washbasin.

For the second time that evening, her feet slipped from under her. This time, she grabbed hold of the shelf. She prevented her own fall, but there was a resounding crash as the mirror came away from the wall, landing in the hand basin and smashing into smithereens.

Heart pounding, and still clutching her ring between forefinger and thumb, she got carefully out of the bath, grabbed her fluffy robe from the back of the door and put it on. As she stared at the shards of glass in the hand basin, she became aware of her entire body trembling and realised she was suffering from shock.

She heard the knock on the bathroom door but couldn't pull herself together to answer before Bryce burst in.

'I didn't let go of my ring. I know it

isn't really a token of love or a promise of togetherness, but I couldn't bear for it to get damaged,' Flora babbled through chattering teeth. 'I know when you have a fiancée for real she'll wear your aunt's ring because you'll choose someone suitable to fall in love with. I know I wouldn't be suitable, I'm not good enough to be part of the Torman . . . Bryce, what are you doing?'

'Carrying you into the living room, and then I'll get you some brandy for shock,' he said.

Flora looped her arms around his neck as he lifted her. 'Like it in your arms,' she whispered, nuzzling her face against his soft jumper. 'But any relationship between us wouldn't be right. You told me that years ago, didn't you?'

Bryce made no response to that as he strode into the living room and lowered her onto the sofa. And when he did speak, it was only to ask if there was a duvet on her bed. It was an effort, but she managed to nod a reply.

'I'll be back with it in two ticks,' he said. 'Brandy?' he asked once he'd covered her with the duvet.

'Small table over there.' Flora pointed. After she'd swallowed a couple of drops, she said, 'You know what they say about breaking a mirror. Do you think I'll have seven years of bad luck now? Maybe if I do go to Holland and set up flower boutiques for Gurth Godwin, they'll be doomed. Maybe I shouldn't go away in the New Year. Maybe I should brave it out and stay here . . . '

Bryce changed from being gentle and caring to sounding annoyed and brusque. 'I turned the bacon and mushrooms off when I heard the crash, and I hadn't started the eggs. I'll go and sort things out. We'll eat, then you can tell me who the heck Gurth Godwin is and what you meant by maybe not going to Holland. I'd no idea you were even contemplating doing that.'

Bryce took a few deep breaths as he walked out of the living room and back into Flora's kitchen. He was amazed at the feeling of despair that had filled him at the thought of Flora possibly going away. Although she'd babbled something about not being able to bear for the ring to get damaged, that didn't mean she'd suddenly come to care for *him* the way he had for her.

And why should she consider herself unsuitable for him to fall in love with? He knew now he loved her truly and deeply. Must have done all along really. Look how he'd wanted to put his arms around her and hold her tight when he thought Harvey Illingworth had done or said something to hurt her — and how disgusted and angry he'd been with the way Harvey had drawn unwelcome attention to her at the auction. It had taken him all his restraint not to flatten that upstart instead of just escorting him from the premises.

He was positive any feelings Flora might once have had for Harvey were long dead and buried, but he couldn't bear the thought of her maybe having any for this Gurth Godwin, whoever he was — or for cousin Rupert who, Bryce remembered grimly, had been talking about the possibility of setting up a showroom in Holland.

Yes, he was sorry for himself — suffering from unrequited love. But after cursing under his breath, Bryce told himself to 'man up' and accept the fact that his gorgeous, lovable, annoying, volatile pretend-fiancée would never be his to . . . He recalled the words he'd listened to at Val and Quentin's wedding rehearsal. Flora would never be his to 'love, honour, comfort and protect' — and she must never find out how much he wanted her to be, he ordered himself firmly as he reached for the eggs.

Once all the food was ready he put it on warmed plates, put the plates on a tray and, hoping he could make himself look nonchalant, carried it through to the living room. Flora swivelled around and swung her feet to the ground. There would have been room for him to sit next to her while they ate but he placed the tray across her knees, picked up his own plate and went to sit on a chair at the side of the hearth.

'This is delicious, thank you, Bryce,' she said after a few seconds.

He nodded. Although he'd been really hungry when they'd first returned from carol singing, his recent self-revelations had stolen his appetite, and the food could have been sawdust for all the enjoyment he was getting out of it.

And, Flora, in spite of having told him it was delicious, seemed to have lost her appetite too, because shaking her head and apologising to him, she said she couldn't finish the food.

Relieved he didn't feel the need to struggle to finish his own now, he stood up. 'Not to worry. I'll clear everything away and then make a cup of hot chocolate.'

By the time he walked back into the living room with their drinks, Flora was curled up under the duvet fast asleep. She looked so cosy, so relaxed, he didn't have the heart to wake her. Returning to the kitchen, he found a paper bag and wrote a message: 'Will pick you up around 7 in the morning.' He propped the note against a book on a small occasional table in the living room where Flora would be sure to spot it when she woke, put a couple more pieces of coal on the fire, made sure it was safe and placed the guard in front of it. He glanced quickly across to make sure she hadn't stirred and, after wishing he had the right to kiss her goodbye, he switched one lamp off, dimmed the other one, walked away and let himself quietly out of her flat.

Walking to his car, he realised the bits of shattered mirror were still in the hand basin in Flora's bathroom. He slowed his steps, wondering if he should go back, but decided it would be best for him if he didn't see Flora again this evening.

Hopefully, things would look better in the morning. He'd still ask her what she'd meant about going or not going to Holland. Maybe, though, after a good night's sleep, he'd find himself with a 'couldn't care less' attitude. And even if she told him she was going there to be with the Gurth Godwin person he'd never heard of, or with Rupert, he'd be able to shrug and ask himself, 'So what?'

13

Flora woke at two in the morning, saw Bryce's note, and the roller-coaster events of the previous day came flooding back. The time spent with the Woodfords, of seeing Bryce, 'Uncle Speckles', with the youngsters, and of him and her taking little Amelia for her nap, was a bittersweet recollection. Skip a few hours and when Bryce had arrived to pick her up to go to his mother's, they'd bickered and snapped, but that had ended in shared laughter.

The next good memory was of joining the carol singers when she and Bryce had spent another couple of hours of harmonious togetherness. Probably the strongest memory of all, though, was the one related to the shattering of the bathroom mirror.

Cripes. She leapt up off the sofa. She knew she hadn't cleared away the broken glass and couldn't recall Bryce doing so, either, unless he'd done it after she'd fallen asleep. On discovering he hadn't, Flora hurried to fetch a dustpan and brush, newspaper to wrap the glass into and a bin bag.

As she took the full bin bag into the kitchen, her mind flew back to Bryce carrying her out of the bathroom; of how she'd babbled on about engagement rings. And had she really told him she liked it in his arms? Maybe he hadn't heard that because he'd been gentle and caring, making her comfy and warm on the sofa, giving her a couple of drops of brandy and . . .

'And then he changed back to his usual unpredictable self after I had mentioned maybe not going to Holland to set up flower boutiques there.' He'd sounded pretty terse when he'd asked who Gurth Godwin was. And because she'd fallen asleep after eating, they hadn't talked about any of that as Bryce had suggested they would. Well, she'd tell him on the way to his mother's as she'd originally planned to do.

* * *

Considering she'd had so little sleep, she didn't look too bad, Flora thought as she put the final touches to her light make-up; in fact she'd scrubbed up well. And when Bryce arrived on the dot of seven, she thought she read approval in those dark eyes taking in her appearance.

However, after saying how last night he'd forgotten about the glass from the mirror until after he'd left, the only other comment he made was, 'Ready?'

After putting on her coat and fetching her shoulder-bag — no overnight bag needed today — Flora calmly agreed she was.

The cold air bit into her and she pulled her coat closer around her. Their footsteps crunched over the thick frost and she felt his fingers curling lightly beneath her elbow, guiding her through the morning darkness as they walked to the car. He'd left it outside the gates again — not only for convenience this time, he explained, but out of consideration for the occupants of the other flats. 'No need to disturb their Sunday slumbers with car doors and engine sounds.'

Never mind if I get frozen to death walking to the car, Flora thought ungraciously, then immediately chided herself for her selfishness.

As if he'd read her thoughts, Bryce murmured, 'Don't worry, the car's nice and warm, and I've brought a sheepskin rug for you to wrap round yourself if you need it.'

One of the nice things about him, Flora acknowledged, as he opened the passenger door and handed her in, placing the rug over her knees, was his inherent courtesy towards other people. Even in these unnatural circumstances, it came through.

His next words further confirmed that thought; for as he slid into the driver's seat, he glanced at her and said,

'I know you're used to early mornings. What I don't know is whether you'd prefer music or peace and quiet while we travel?'

'Has it got to be one of those two?' She spoke softly, trying to make it clear she wasn't being awkward or looking for a scrap.

He regarded her thoughtfully, as if trying to judge her mood.

'Maybe we could talk,' she added, hoping she'd sounded calmer than she felt. His closeness, the drift of his male cologne, his hands on the steering wheel and ignition, were beginning to unsettle her. Hopefully she'd cope better while telling him about Gurth Godwin and the possibility of her setting up flower boutiques for him.

'By all means, talk if you wish,' he agreed as he put the car in motion.

This time his courtesy grated on her nerves; for a wild moment she wished she could disturb his equilibrium.

A short while later, Flora stared at Bryce and recalled an old saying: 'Take care before wishing, lest that wish come true.' Because to her absolute amazement, when she'd detailed her plans for the New Year, he'd turned on her in fury.

'It won't upset your mother,' she'd protested, trying to speak calmly. 'She'd have no idea I was going, because I can't contemplate continuing to pretend you and I are engaged and in love. And even though we'd *still* let her and everyone think we *are* engaged, she'd be the first to agree my career is important — you know she would.'

'I know I can't drive and talk about your preposterous idea at the same time,' he stated. 'I'm sick to death of holding this type of conversation in my car. Just keep quiet until I find somewhere we can get out and walk.'

Flora kept quiet. Not because he'd told her to, but because she was stunned by his unexpected adverseness. Why couldn't he see that she was offering them an ideal way out of their predicament, because when two or three months had gone by they could officially end their 'engagement'? And what was preposterous about working for Gurth Godwin? It was a perfectly sound, extremely lucrative proposition.

'Right, get out, Flora,' he ordered brusquely, and she realised he'd stopped the car at the entrance to Oulton Park, the famous racing circuit.

As she got out of the car, she heard church bells ringing from the nearby village and thought how incongruous they were when she and Bryce were about to embark on a heated discussion. 'No, we're incongruous, not them,' she muttered.

'Your idea of travelling round, setting up flower boutiques for someone else's benefit, certainly is.' Bryce spoke harshly and took a grip of her arm so she had no other choice other than to walk alongside him. She'd no doubt he'd drag her along if she didn't.

'I don't understand you, Bryce,' she protested. 'It's the ideal way out of things and — '

'When did you first meet this Gurth Godwin?'

'I don't know what that's got to do with anything, but I gave a flower-arranging demonstration in one of his hotels I already supplied with plants and flowers. It was very successful, very well attended. Shortly afterwards he approached me with his offer. At the time I turned it down. I — '

'Why? Why did you turn it down? Because you could see he wanted to use your knowledge and expertise for his own benefit, not for — '

'I turned it down for personal reasons. I was going out with Harvey Illingworth at the time. That was before I realised what he was like, and I thought . . . Well, anyway, I turned it down.'

'Your business acumen leaves much to be desired, Flora. You turn an offer down because you think you're in love with one man, then later accept because you think you're in love with my cousin Rupert, who happens to be talking about setting up a showroom in Holland. There isn't really that much to choose between the two men, though I must admit Rupert is more genuine than — '

'No way do I think I'm in love with Rupert, and I'd no idea he was thinking of opening a showroom in Holland. I'd be accepting Gurth's offer because of you, Bryce. Or because of the situation Val and your uncle Hector between them have got us into. And as for Gurth Godwin using me, what the hell do you think you're doing?'

They were following a track between tree-lined verges and, pulling her arm free, Flora moved away to lean against a large and comforting tree trunk.

'What are *you* doing, if not using me?' she asked again.

'All right, Flora, I admit I'm using you. The difference being, it isn't for my own gain.'

'Oh no? What about your inheritance?' Immediately she'd said those words, she wished she hadn't.

Bryce came towards her, placed his hands on her shoulders and gazed down into her eyes.

'I'm sorry,' she groaned. 'I didn't mean that, Bryce. I know your inheritance was the original reason Val gave for everything, but of course I also know you didn't want to go along with her plan for any reason at first.'

'I'm sorry, too. Sorry for everything. Maybe accepting Gurth Godwin's offer would be a good thing after all. But, Flora sweetheart, like I said, I don't like the idea of you using your knowledge, your expertise your creativity, for someone else's benefit.'

Bryce sounded as if he really meant it; sounded as if he cared. To her bewilderment, Flora became aware of tears trickling down her cheeks.

She heard Bryce swear under his breath as he wiped the tears away with his thumbs. 'Hell, Flora, I don't like the idea of you spending time away from your flat and Torman Hall. I don't like the idea of us ending our engagement

— fake though it is.'

'That's crazy, Bryce. Even if you happened to have feelings for me, nothing could ever come of it. I think the main reason your mother and your uncle seem pleased to think we're engaged is because I'm not Jilly Joy.'

'Thank the lord for that,' Bryce said. 'Agreeing to keep an eye on her for her parents was one of the worst decisions I've ever had the misfortune to make. Still, I think she's taken herself off my radar now and is interested in one of her fellow actors.'

'I wish them both luck,' Flora said. 'I just hope the poor actor doesn't come from a family that can't afford any scandals.'

'Having her out of my hair could, if we were storybook characters, give me a chance to concentrate on trying to convince you that I wish our engagement could be real, because my feelings for you are. And — '

'I don't know why you're saying things like this, Bryce. I've told you why your mother and uncle seem to approve, but *you* don't think I'm suitable to become a member of the Torman family. You said yourself that any kind of relationship between you, the heir to the Torman Estate, and me, the daughter of an estate worker, wouldn't be right.'

He took a step back, an unmistakeable look of shock and horror on his face. 'Flora, I know I've said a few things in my time to wind you up, but I'm sure I have never said anything so crass, cruel, and so untrue to boot.'

'That night in the barn when I was hiding a present for Val and I fell from the hayloft — and you, who should have been at the opera, broke my fall. And . . . '

'And you started to kiss me.'

Flora felt her face turn warm and looked down at her feet so Bryce wouldn't see her discomfort. 'Fancy you remembering that,' she said, trying for sarcasm, but as her voice had come out husky, guessing she'd failed.

'You've no idea how many times I've thought about that evening. As I recall, you didn't let me finish what I'd started to say. You weren't quite sixteen, Flora, and I was twenty-five. I don't suppose you can imagine what a hell of an effort it was not to kiss you senseless.'

'Really?' she mumbled, and an unexpected warmth surged through her.

'Oh, yes. Really. Until then I'd tried telling myself that anything I felt for you was brotherly love, but I think I knew that even though you were so young, what I felt was . . . Anyway, any relationship between us at that stage would not have been right. For one reason and one reason only. Because of your age. Not because you were the daughter of someone who worked in the estate offices.'

'Even so, you thought the ring your aunt bequeathed you for your future wife was too good to — '

'God, Flora. I wouldn't want that anywhere near you. It's an ostentatious monster of a thing. Cold and totally devoid of any message of love.'

He sounded so genuine, so . . . so desperate almost, to make her believe him. She lifted her head and gazed into his eyes. 'If only you knew what hurt, what heartbreak those words 'it wouldn't be right' caused, Bryce. Not just at the time but for ever afterwards.'

'Does that mean there's hope for us, Flora? Because my words wouldn't have caused heartbreak if you didn't care for me. Would they?'

The hope and tenderness in his eyes reached her very soul. She looped her arms around his neck and pulled his face down to hers. 'Do you still want to kiss me senseless?' she whispered against his lips.

'You'll never know how much I want to do that, never know how much I love you.'

'Show me then, show me and tell me . . . '

* * *

'Standing under a leafless tree in the middle of winter isn't exactly a romantic setting for a declaration of love,' Bryce said some time later.

'We had our love to keep us warm, though,' Flora murmured. 'Maybe we should make a move. Your mother will be waiting, and — '

'And you mustn't keep your future mother-in-law waiting, must you? Because she is that, isn't she, sweetheart? You *are* going to marry me, aren't you? I won't object if you really want to go and set up the flower boutiques, as long as — '

'I was only thinking of going because it was hurting too much having to pretend to the family I loved you and having to pretend to you I didn't. I might want to open another one or two flower boutiques here. But on the other hand, once the babies come along . . . You do want children, don't you, Bryce?'

'Mmm, dozens.' He laughed. 'But we'd better get married first, my love. Let's fix a date for as soon as possible after Val and Quentin have had their happy day.'

'Valentine's Day,' Flora said dreamily. 'And I'll send you a card for real with 'Love and a million kisses'.' Bryce hugged her as he quoted the words she'd once pretended he'd written.

'I was crying for the moon then,' she said. 'Now I'll never have to do that again.'

A HEART'S WAGER

Heidi Sullivan

Eva Copperfield has lived a life of poverty in the squalid slums of New York — until a sudden inheritance gives her the chance of a new life as lady of the manor in the English countryside. Her journey from rags to riches is complicated by the mysterious Ben — who is either a lord or a charlatan! Eva has to navigate the Atlantic and her heart before she can find a home . . . and love. Wagers are being made. Who will win?